Et

MW01134716

*An anthology of science fiction and fantasy stories
by R. L. Copple*

Published by Ethereal Press
Marble Falls, TX

ISBN: 1-456-50680-3
EAN13: 978-1-456-50680-3

Cover photo courtesy of NASA.

All the characters in this book are fictitious, and any resemblance to actual persons, living or dead, is purely coincidental.

Table of Contents

Forward

After writing science fiction and fantasy stories for the past five years, I realized I have enough of them to put into a book. So enclosed herein you will find the short stories and flash fictions that I've written. Most of these have appeared in online magazines such as *Dragons, Knights and Angels, The Sword Review, Digital Dragon, Resident Aliens, A Thousand Faces, Ray Gun Revival*, among others. A few of these have never been published before, either because to date they have never found a home, or because I only tried once or twice, but I still feel they are stories people would enjoy.

Theme? Nothing really. This isn't so much a themed anthology as a compilation of the stories I've written from 2006 through 2010. The reader will find some adventure, some humor, spoofs, and surreal stories lurking in these pages. This makes a great book for reading at lunch, or while waiting. Most all of these stories will be enjoyed by young readers as well as adults.

The first stories in each section are also firsts for me. "The Call of Nature" in the science fiction section was my first accepted story. *Ray Gun Revival* magazine accepted it in June 2006. However, it wasn't the first published because there was a long delay between its acceptance and when it actually went to print in January 2007. The first story in the fantasy section, "Dragon Stew," takes the honors of being my first published piece, appearing in *Dragons, Knights and Angels* in September, 2006.

But what I've always enjoyed are fun stories, and that has always been my goal. Sure, you may learn a little along the way. Sometimes there are important themes embedded in the stories. But if they aren't fun to read, then that matters little, because few would want to read them. If they offer some joy and brightening of an otherwise dreary day, then my goals have been accomplished.

I offer these in the hope they will do just that. Enjoy the ride. It is rarely ever boring.

R. L. Copple

Science Fiction Stories

The Call of Nature

The metal hanger, which housed the Z-14X prototype space plane, shined in the moonlight just beyond the barbed-wired fence. The moonlight reminded John of the sun. He couldn't wait to see it against the blackness of space.

The security fence gloated, "Just try to get through," but it hadn't counted on someone who could simply fly over. It hadn't counted on— Moth Man.

The only real ability John possessed: he could fly using the soft wings on his back. That and the fact if someone ate him, they would die of toxic poison. "A lot of good that would do me. Why couldn't a radioactive spider have bitten me? Why a moth?" he had often wondered.

Yet now the wings came in handy. He lifted himself into the air. Wind flowed through his hair as he bounced though the cool night over the compound. Soon he sank to the ground beside the hanger.

John peered into the window and saw the craft bathed in dim moonlight: a black shell, adorned by four wings well back on the craft, spread out in an "X" pattern. Just as his web research had revealed. Touted as the first plane to fly successfully out of earth's gravity and into space, it looked the part.

A growl sounded. He swung around to see a German Shepherd baring its teeth. He froze. *I could probably fly away before he reached me.* He prepared to launch.

"Freeze!" A uniformed man swung around the corner, brandishing a rifle pointed straight at John. He froze again.

I might be able to escape the dog, but not the bullet. "Sorry, can you tell me how to get to the Hilton? I seem to be lost."

He didn't buy it. "Up against the wall, hands high." The dog threatened with a low rumbling growl.

John complied, what else could he do? As he followed the officer's orders, his black and gold tiger-moth wings came into view.

"What the…" The officer moved closer and felt the wings. He rubbed the wing dust off his hands with a grimace and then patted John down for weapons.

John saw his opportunity. He swung his wings hard, hitting the officer in the head. The hit and wing dust disoriented him. John's fist landed a hit squarely on the back of his neck. The guard dropped unconscious. John launched himself into the air before the dog could reach him. The Shepherd's snapping jaws just missed John's dangling foot.

The barking dog now broadcasted the fact that an intruder had penetrated the compound. John no longer had time for subtleties. Landing on the roof, he kicked in the skylight. It shattered open, and he winged his way inside.

Now, where did they store the plutonium fuel rods? John swung around and spotted them, in a box labeled as such along the wall. He grabbed a handful and flew to the cockpit. Once inside, he inserted all but two fuel rods into the power receptors and initiated the injection process.

By now, several guards filed in the door, guns encircled the ship. The engines had power, so John increased the throttle. The plane lurched forwards. Gunfire echoed in the hanger. Warning shots, hoping it would scare John into stopping no doubt. They didn't want to riddle their craft with holes. Not until they had no other recourse.

Doing a standard take-off would take too long. John thought about going right to the nuclear escape engines. Such force, designed for airborne ignition, could tear it and him apart from a near-dead stop. He had only one viable course of action.

He braced himself, then hit the ignition switch. The Gs slammed him into the seat. He struggled to maintain consciousness. The metal groaned under the strain. The plane shot forward and ploughed through the hanger doors. Scraping metal sounds echoed through the cockpit. It bounced along the ground. A fence raced toward the plane. John pulled back on the stick, already speeding past 200 knots. The prototype shot upward. The Gs squished him as if a giant hand pushed on his head.

As the plane cleared the buildings and the land quickly receded, John cut the ignition and switched to standard fuel. His field of vision returned and his face reshaped to its rounded state like a baby fresh out of the womb.

John glanced at the escape-engine fuel gauge. The stunt had expended a third of what he needed to escape earth's gravity. He inserted the other two rods. The solar panels should keep life support going as long as needed. John didn't expect to return anyway.

John released manual control to the computer. The escape engines fired. Again he sank into the seat. The craft angled higher. The blue sky receded. The stars brightened, looking like white sand dusting a black void. The horizon shifted to a curved surface rimmed with the sun's golden silhouette.

Suddenly, a ray of sunlight broke over the earth's rim, bathing John in awe. Its beauty filled his mind. The light entranced John; its song called to him.

Time suspended, the shinning light against the blackness of space filled all desire. Before, John had flown as high as his wings would let him but the sun remained out of reach. Now, he could soar until he soaked in all of its beautiful light.

John pulled a disk from his pocket and held it before his eyes. He had pre-programmed the flight path: a one-way trip to the sun. His gaze moved back to the enveloping fireball. He could hold back no longer. John slid the disk into the ship's computer. It responded with beeps and a message reading, "program accepted." The engines adjusted the trajectory.

Did John know it would kill Him? Yes. But he didn't care. He could not rest until he took in all the glorious radiance his body could endure.

"Why couldn't I have been bit by a radioactive spider instead?"

Spaced Out
Starry Mysteries

"Time for our next mission." Starry Skyward held his wrist-vid up.

Tramal arched her bald head closer to listen. "About time. We'll dock with the *Armageddon* soon."

Her scent rose from sweat beading on her neck. He didn't know why, but it always smelled sweet to him. His attention drifted to the beauty of her translucent skin and the gentle pulses of her spine-ridges through her thin blouse. "I'm feeling a little hot. Are you hot?"

She cracked a smile. "Aren't I always?"

Dolan cleared his throat. "Mind if I join the party?"

Starry jumped and looked at his wrist-vid. He felt his cheeks flush. Dolan's chubby face, surrounded by a thin film of sandy hair, filled the screen.

"Sorry, Boss." Starry cleared his throat. "What's up?"

"Explosions, that's what."

Starry glanced at Tramal. "You suspect the *Armageddon* will be next?"

"Yes. The Planetary Intelligence Tribunal believes the *Armageddon* is the next target of the terrorists."

Starry twisted his mouth. "Inside job?"

"We believe so. Most likely one of the groups out to destroy the Plenary Organization of Planets."

"It's easy to gin up support against POoP, but dang hard to find anyone for it."

Dolan frowned. "Starry, do you know how many of those jokes I've heard? We get those comments all the time from the public, I don't need my agents shoving it in my face too."

"Sorry, Sir. But they should have considered that when they named the organization. I do stand-up for a living you know, can't help it."

"You're an agent for a living, the stand-up is your cover. Keep it straight." Dolan narrowed his eyes.

"Yes, Sir."

Tramal sighed. "Can we get back to the mission, guys?"

"My wife's right, let's flush the POoP and get back to the mission."

Dolan rolled his eyes. "We believe one rebel integrates himself into the crew and gains access to sensitive engine areas. He disables the fusion containment collective, allowing the fusion process to burn out of control and destroy the ship. They all have the marks of an inside job, which is disturbing."

"I'll say," Starry said. "Your filtering of recruits leaves something to be desired."

Dolan leaned over his desk. "Leave the recruiting process to others. Your mission is to find this saboteur before he blows up another ship. Got it?"

"Yes, Sir," they both said.

"Good. Make contact once you're off the ship. Transmission ended." The screen blanked out.

Tramal placed a hand on his knee. "Why do you antagonize him?"

"You're touching me. Read my mind why don't you?"

"I can only get impressions of intentions that way. I know you're enjoying his reactions, but why is my question."

Leave it to a Hilmosian to make that distinction. "It's an Academy thing. You would've had to have been there to appreciate it."

Her face color flowed from pale gold to a light blue—her business mode. "We'll be docking within two minutes, and we still need to plan our strategy."

Starry craned his neck to the port window. He could see the *Armageddon's* polished hull glancing beams of sunlight into space. A thin body running through a hollow tube rotated on a magnetic track. Two engines flared from the outer hull and one from the back of the main body. "Well, I suggest we go in, track down the bad guy, and take him or her out."

"What kind of plan is that? Do I always have to come up with the plans?"

He smiled. "Why do you think we make such a good team? You plan, I execute."

"Yeah. Right."

The ship docked. Air locks locked. Soon they entered the receiving hall of the *Armageddon*. The Captain and officers awaited them amidst metal so clean Starry could see his reflection waver as it followed them. Echoes of his and Tramal's boots reverberated through the high-ceilinged room, leaving the impression of a sparse life aboard the starship.

The Captain stretched out a hand. "Welcome aboard. I'm Captain Raleigh." He nodded to the man next to him. "This is Commander Speller, my second-in-command. He oversees the operational administration of the ship."

The Commander frowned, as if he would rather they weren't there, but nodded.

Starry nodded back. "Looks like you could use some laughs on this ship."

The captain chuckled and slapped the stoic Commander on the back. "Yes, we could use some laughs. We've been through a lot the last several months heightened by the fear of blowing-up at any moment. I can't wait to hear your routine."

Tramal reached out a hand to the Commander. "Do you think the saboteur is here?"

The Commander hesitated, then shook her hand. "No ma'am, I'm sure he isn't."

"Commander, show these people to their quarters."

He saluted. "Aye, Captain." Then he turned and proceeded down the hall. "Follow me."

"You can put the luggage over there." Tramal pointed to a corner.

Three ensigns dragged the suitcases into the room and dropped them in a pile. The last one, huffing and sweating. "You have a lot of luggage, Ma'am."

Starry cupped his palm to one side of his mouth. "Guess you've never been married before, have you?"

"No, Sir."

"While single, you are a pack rat, but once you are married, you become a pack mule."

"Good one, Sir." He exited the room.

"I would say pretty lame. I hope you have better stuff tonight."

"Hey, I can't give my best stuff away before the show."

Her lips turned up. "Oh, the responses I could say to that. You're wide open."

Starry checked his zipper then pointed a finger at her. "Be nice."

She pulled out a small rectangular device from a suitcase. "Have I ever been any other way?" Before he could answer, she pushed a button and screaming hard rock music blasted through the room. She rotated around, bopping to the beat, and then sauntered to a spot next to a mirror on the wall. The unit had uncovered an eavesdropping portal. She slid out the back of the unit a nearly transparent film and stuck it over the wall where a bare pinprick could be seen.

The film replaced themselves with pre-recorded images of them sleeping, chatting, taking baths and the like. Computer scans would integrate the images with the current room layout whenever they were in the room.

She continued scanning while Starry finished unpacking until she had found them all. Then she shut the music off; they could talk freely.

Starry sat in a chair by the table and ordered a glass of tea from the computer. "Specify kind," the computer responded.

"Chamomile, iced, no sugar."

"Thank you, your beverage will arrive in one minute and ten seconds."

"Computers leave out all the mystery."

"Speaking of mystery, I didn't detect any attempts to deceive from the Captain."

"And the Commander?"

"He didn't like us here...I felt he hid something. He's one to watch."

"Bring up his service record."

Tramal tapped on her wrist-vid. "Says he's been with the ship for five years now."

Starry scratched his head. "Can't be him then. Who has signed on recently?"

"The Chief Engineer and an Ensign assigned to navigation."

"Either of them previously assigned to the *Bolgart*?" Starry waited patiently while she searched. The *Bolgart* had been the last of five ships to go down.

"Hum, yes. The Chief Engineer. His name is Chris Stanson."

"Bingo!" *This could prove to be an easy assignment.* "Let me see his photo."

She held her wrist-vid to his eyes. "Why don't we go eat in the mess hall. Maybe we'll spot him."

The door light lit up and beeped. "Right after I've had my tea, Babe. Have a seat."

———

Chatter filled the mess hall: a long narrow room full of tables and chairs bolted to the floor met a counter dividing the dining area from the kitchen. Metal covered every inch, giving the room an impersonal feel. Nevertheless, people clustered around tables offset the Spartan atmosphere.

Starry and Tramal filled their trays with the day's special. To his pleasure, Starry discovered the chief engineer at a table by himself. He pointed at him for Tramal to follow.

"Is this seat taken?" Starry put his hand on its back and waited for Chris to respond.

"Go ahead, I just sat down myself." He didn't bother to raise his head.

"Thanks. My name's Starry, by the way, and this is my wife, Tramal." They sat their food down and pulled themselves up to the table.

"Oh, the funny guy, right?" He glanced up at Starry and then checked out Tramal. "You're a Hilmosian, aren't you?"

"Yes, I am. And you're an Earthling, aren't you?" She held out her hand.

"Yes. Obviously." Instead of shaking hands, he dropped his gaze down to his plate. He hadn't taken a bite but seemed to be playing with his food.

"Hey, there's something in your ear." Starry reached over and pulled a coin from it and tacked a tracking device onto the back of his ear. "Now you're rich. Don't spend it all in one place." He tossed the coin onto the table. It rolled until it fell to a circling stop.

"Cute trick, but old."

Starry shrugged his shoulders and examined Chris's meal. "Yum, smells good. What is it?"

Chris put some on his fork, raised it to his nose, and sniffed. "Seaweed salad with the 'house' dressing. Looked better at the counter."

"Wow, brings back memories. I grew up on seaweed salad. Botanically grown on the ship, right?"

"He grew up on a space ship." Tramal stuffed a forkful of fish into her mouth.

"Here, you can have it. I'm not hungry."

"Thanks!" Starry dragged the plate to himself and filled his mouth with the salty leaves. "Pretty good. My mom cooked it better, but still, pretty good."

"I don't suppose you've heard any recent news about the *Bolgart* have you?" Tramal paused for a moment, awaiting his response.

"Me? No. Why would I have any news?" Chris's eyes darted around and then he focused on his hands.

"Mess halls are where we get our news. Kind of grass roots level, you know."

"Why not news-vids?"

"They only tell you what POoP wants you to hear. You get the real low down here."

"Or a lot of bloated opinion." He rose from the table. "Sorry to leave you, but I have duties to attend to. Hope your show goes well."

Starry swallowed a mouthful of seaweed. "You aren't attending?"

"Sorry, I have station duty tonight. I'll have to catch a different show. Now, if you'll pardon me..." He nodded and stepped through the hall and out the door.

"Well, I don't have to be a Hilmosian to read his body language. You see how he reacted when you brought up the topic?"

She nodded. "What I'm more worried about is tonight while you're doing the show would be a perfect time for him to set off the reactors."

"At least it means I could go out with a bang."

Tramal rubbed her forehead.

He shrugged. "Okay, during the act, why don't you track him and keep an eye on him. If he starts messing with the reactors, take him out."

"That'll go over good: 'But Captain, your engineer worked on the engines so I took him out.'"

Starry winked at her. "Just don't blow our cover."

"But you said I plan, you execute. What happened to that?"

"Well, you know. I've got a show people are dying to hear."

She groaned. "Just finish your seaweed before I cram it down your throat."

A crowd filled the rec-room. Starry noticed the Captain and Commander, grim as ever, at a front table. He spotted Tramal slipping out the back door. He knew she could handle herself, but he worried anyway. He sucked in a deep breath as a man on the narrow stage introduced him.

"And now, here he is, Starry the Space Hippie!"

He bounded onto the stage and waited for the clapping to die down. "I grew up with some groovy parents. Dad would always say, 'Yeah man, we're really far out now!'

"We traveled on several space ships, wherever we could hitch a ride. I had free love and free trouble..."

Starry entered their room after the show. Tramal sat at the table staring into her wrist-vid.

"Well, the show's over and I'm still alive. How did it go?"

She sighed. "He worked on the thrust engines all night. Never came close to the fusion reactors. Then his shift ended and he left to get some zees." She held her wrist-vid for him to see. "Right now, he's in his quarters."

"I'll bet he is the one, though. He's just playing his hand carefully. We might have aroused his something's-not-right radar at supper." Starry stretched and yawned. "I'm ready for dreamland."

"Not without me you don't." She stood up and grabbed him around the waist, then pulled his lips into hers for a few seconds.

Starry reveled in the familiar warmth and love. They broke for air. "I hoped I would meet you in my dreams."

"Who said I was talking about dreams?" She kissed him as they fell onto the bed.

"Take your hands off those controls or we'll fire!"

Starry shook his head. He felt cold. As his eyes focused, he realized he stood in the engine room with his hands on the fusion reactor control panel.

"What the...?" He examined himself. Not one piece of clothing covered his body. "What am I doing here?"

"That's what we want to know. Step away or we fire."

Starry glanced around. Several guards with Erupter-class ray-rifles surrounded him. He backed away and held his hands up. "I don't suppose anyone has a spare set of clothes?"

"Mind telling us, funny guy, why you're in the engine room initiating a containment field shutdown?"

Starry shrugged. "Honestly, I don't know. If I had planned this, do you think I would 'sneak' in naked? Give me a little more credit."

Chris entered the room and stopped when he saw Starry. First his face fell, but then his jaw firmed and his eyes narrowed. "So, you're the one who killed all my friends. You no account, son of..." He shot towards Starry.

Several of the guards grabbed him but not before Starry ducked a swinging fist. They pulled Chris back.

"Seriously, I didn't do it." Starry felt desperation take over. He couldn't be locked up while the real killer still roamed the ship. But how did he get here? Why was he shutting down the containment field? He didn't even know how to shut down a containment field.

"You lying dog!" Chris struggled to free himself from the guard's grip. "You're caught in the act."

"He's right," the head-guard said. He motioned with his rifle. "Time to lock you up. We already have guards going to arrest your wife and accomplice. We tracked her studying the engine room layout last night. Obviously you two are a team. A team that will now be out of business, thankfully."

Starry slumped. "Can I at least get some clothes from my room? I'm a little cold." Goosebumps covered his arms. "Not to mention some of these guards seem to be staring a little too longingly at me."

The head-guard shook his head. "Always the comedian to the end, eh? Now you can entertain the executioner." He examined Starry with a grimace. "But first, we'll drop by your room to cover up this sorry excuse for a body."

Several rifles followed Starry as he exited the room. He hoped none of the guards carried enough resentment to take it out on him. They would probably get no more than a slap on the hand for killing the "saboteur."

But, more disturbing, Chris didn't act like someone who had blown-up the *Bogart* much less planned to take out the *Armageddon*. Either he had pegged the wrong man or Chris put on good act. If an act, they would all die soon. If they thought they had caught the real criminal, he could finish the job unhindered.

The door to his quarters slid open. The leader pointed to two of his three men. "You two, guard the door."

"Ay, Sir," they said in unison and took up positions on either side.

He shoved Starry into his room, ray-rifle still trained on his head. "Get on your clothes and don't go slow. We'll start going through your luggage while we wait." The door closed behind them.

"Sure, why not. Just don't open the green one over there." Starry pointed at the pile. "It's my wife's and she doesn't like people going through her stuff."

The two men exchanged grins and chuckled. "Why don't we start with that one?"

"Okay, but don't say I didn't warn you." Starry opened his suitcase and grabbed the filter nose-plugs.

"Where's the latch on this one?" One of the men had it in the air, rotating it to get a better view.

"See the hole by the latch? Stick your finger in and it'll open right up." Starry shoved the plugs firmly in.

"Oh, I see it." He stuck his finger in the hole. A gas shot into their faces and they collapsed onto the floor in a twisted pile of bodies.

"Cool, works every time." He reached down to straighten the men out. "You can come out now, Babe."

A larger suitcase unlatched and opened. Tramal stretched. "Thank goodness, my joints ached in there. The computer warned of a forced entry and I—" She stopped upon spotting him naked. "Who was she?"

"No one. I woke up at the controls of the fusion reactor, in the process of shutting down the containment field. One minute I'm going to sleep in your arms, next I'm standing naked in front of several armed guards. Like I sleep-walked or something."

"Really?" She put her chin in her right hand. "It wasn't meant for you. Don't you see, the rebels use mind control to explode the ships. They must have meant to control someone who wouldn't arouse suspicions. Like one of the crew who works here."

Starry scratched his head. "And somehow I ended up with it by accident. But how? The members of the crew I had contact with were the Captain, the Commander, and Chris, the Chief Engineer."

Tramal's eyes widened. "The salad. The cook prepared it for the chief engineer, but you ate it instead. There had to be Delirium in the dressing."

"Delirium? You're saying I'm crazy?" Starry began undressing the two guards.

"Well, I'm not saying you're not crazy, but no, not in this instance. Delirium is a chemical used to control people. By coding the chemical signatures, it creates the pathways in the brain's subconscious to carry out commands at a pre-determined time."

"How come you know so much about this? You haven't used it on me, have you?" Starry pulled the guard's pants around his own waist and buckled the belt.

She winked at him. "Maybe, maybe not. I'm not telling."

"Tramal!"

"Don't you think we had better focus on the task at hand? If I heard correctly, we have two guards outside our door, two asleep in here, and a scant few minutes to clear our names." She tucked the guard's uniform-shirt into her pants.

Starry jerked his shoes on harder than needed. "Yeah, right. Ignore the issue. Meanwhile, why don't you send those guys back an hour in time while I create the masks."

She pulled what appeared to be a flashlight from her suitcase. "One hour it is," she said as she dialed it in. Then she put the unit on the forehead, back, and sides of each head. A red light glowed while on one spot, and she moved it to the next location when it turned green. "The last hour of their lives never existed. No tattletaling for them."

Starry unwrapped a sheet of mask paper and laid it over the head-guard's face. He shined the red activating-light onto the paper and it molded into a perfect replica. He peeled the mask off and carefully placed it onto his own face. "Did you get the recording of the head-guard while you were in the suitcase?"

"Yeah, here." She held her wrist-vid close to his mask and tapped on the screen a few times. "There, say something."

"Do you ever go out with other men?"

"Perfect, you sound just like him. And no, I don't. Nor do I stalk the ship at night, naked, scaring everyone." She accepted the mask from him and placed it securely onto her face.

"You should try it sometime. A real hoot." He chuckled. "Here, put this cap on."

"Thanks. Tie those two up and I'll prepare our alibi."

"Oh? What alibi?"

She lifted a vial into view. "Delirium, of course."

"I knew you were using that!"

"Every good undercover agent has to use all tools at their disposal." She put a drop into a small box and held it to her wrist-vid. "But no, I've not used this on you. This stuff cost too much."

"Oh, so now I'm not worth it, is that it?"

She put the box on the table and tapped her screen. "Now, Dear, you're worth it." She grabbed his face with her free hand and shook it back and forth. "But I don't need it to control you." The box beeped.

Starry twisted his mouth into a frown. "I give up."

Tramel smirked. "See?"

Starry shook his head. "So, what did you program the Delirium to do?"

"Once injected, it directs the person to go straight to a computer and download all information he or she knows about the sabotage plans via voice recording and send it to headquarters."

He took the injector from her, filled with the drop. "Just as good as a confession."

"But make sure we get it into the person who put the chemical into the dressing, or we'll be sending a worthless confession to headquarters."

"The guards are tied, gagged, and under the covers. They won't have a clue when they wake up."

She shoved the cap well down her head. "So, they're undercover guards."

"Hey, I was going to say that."

"I know. You're way too predictable." She pecked his cheek.

Starry sighed and slid his cap into place. "Let's go."

The door slid open and they stepped through. Starry faced the guards. "We've had a change of plans. We have bound them and put them on the beds. They're confined to quarters. Don't let anyone in or out with a rank lower than mine."

"Aye, Sir."

Starry and Tramal marched to the kitchen.

Starry slipped through the open doors into the Mess Hall. Several people milled around; various groups of crew members sat at tables eating. He glanced at Tramal. "How are we going to know who the culprit is?"

"Deductive reasoning, my dear Starry." She winked.

Nothing to do but take the direct approach. He moved to the order counter. A young man approached them.

"Where's the head-cook, Scrub?"

"Just a second, I'll get her." He scurried to the back.

Five seconds passed before she came out with the young man on her heals. "Yes, what can I do for you?"

"What's in your house salad-dressing?"

The cook's brow wrinkled. "Well, the usual. Oil, salt, pepper, oregano, a little lemon spice."

"Any 'secret' ingredients?"

She cocked an eye at him. "Planning on starting a competing brand, are we, Jarrel?"

"No. I can taste something, but I can't put my finger on it. I can't sleep thinking about it."

"Poor baby." She patted Starry's cheek. "Guess you aren't going to get much sleep for a while, are you?"

This trail led to a brick wall, but she ranked as the most likely suspect. He would have to take the risk, their window would soon close. He waved her closer. "I'll let you in on my secret."

She leaned over and Starry reached for her shoulder as he drew near to her ear, palming the injector.

Doubt flooded over him. He couldn't inject her. "Pssst, it's a secret: I can't tell you," he whispered in her ear.

She pulled back with her hands on her hips, a frown on her face.

"Guard Jarrel!" a commanding voice rang out. The Mess Hall buzz abruptly died.

It took Starry a moment before he responded, forgetting he wore Jarrel's face and clothes. The Captain and the Commander approached him. Starry stood straight and saluted. "Yes, Sir."

"I don't recall receiving any reports on the status of the two who were arrested? Why are you in the Mess Hall getting something to eat?" The Captain asked.

"I wasn't, Sir. I was...investigating."

"Investigating what?"

"My house dressing," the head-cook said.

The Commander's face reddened.

The Captain's eyes narrowed and his face grew stern. "Let's go to the holding cell where the captives are, Guard. You'll give your report to us there."

"But Sir, I had a valid reason for wanting to know about the salad dressing."

"Out with it then."

Starry felt the eyes in the room staring at him. "It's classified, could you two come in close?"

The Commander grunted and frowned, but drew in with the Captain. Starry put his right hand on the Commander's neck and shot the chemical into him. He flinched as if a fly had landed on his neck, but said nothing.

"I have reason to believe the house dressing was spiked with a chemical."

The Commander gritted his teeth. "We've caught the ones who are exploding ships all over the fleet, and you're investigating chemicals in a house dressing? Your orders are to take care of the criminals we did catch. Move it!"

"Yes, Sir."

The Captain and Commander followed behind Starry and Tramal in silence. A few seconds ticked by as they turned down one hall, and then another.

"Stop," the Captain said.

Starry turned back and saw the Commander approaching a com console. The chemical had taken effect. But what would he say?

"Patch through to headquarters and send the following message. This is Commander Arnold, second-in-command of the starship *Armeggedon* currently assigned to the *Corona Cluster*. Concerning the sabotage of several vessels of our fleet, I do not know who has conducted these operations."

Starry shook his head. They were dead meat now. Do we gas the Captain and the Commander and tie them up too? He glanced at Tramal and her eyes told him she didn't have any idea how they would get out of this either.

"However," the Commander continued, "I do have knowledge of the method employed. Coded Delirium is injected into the food of someone assigned to engineering. The code activates the victim at a specified time to shut down the fusion containment field, creating a breach and subsequent explosion of the ship."

The Captain's eyes were as big as golf balls and his mouth hung open. Starry gave Tramal the thumbs up sign.

"Additionally, I had been drugged, most likely at the Academy, so I would add Delirium to the house dressing of the chief engineer's salad to disable the fusion containment field."

Starry's mouth fell open. He saw Tramal's face light up. "Jackpot."

"Jackpot, indeed." The Captain whirled around. I'm sorry Guard Jarrel. You were on the money with this one. You'll be getting a huge promotion out of this. I would never have guessed. But how did you get him to confess?"

"Found some of his Delirium, and re-coded it to use against him. I knew I had to be sneaky about it as long as he ranked me."

"I'm highly impressed with your work. Obviously our comedian guest was a victim of this drug instead of the culprit. We're lucky he ended up with it instead of someone from engineering. We wouldn't have had a chance."

"Right, Sir." They both saluted. "With your permission, I'll take Commander Arnold into custody until we can determine if he is safe, and I'll free the two we have in custody. We'll also need to initiate scans on all food supplies for Delirium."

"Yes, yes, by all means. Carry on." The Captain turned and left.

Starry wrapped hand restraints around the Commander's wrists and headed toward the holding cells with his new prisoner.

"How did you know the Commander did it and not the cook?" Tramal asked after they had deposited the Commander in his cell and headed back to their room.

"Elementary, my dear Tramal. Body language. The cook told me she didn't do it, but the Commander did. Knowing he oversaw the administration of the ship, including food supplies, and you had sensed he hid something, his reaction to me said, 'I'm guilty' as if he had it written on his forehead."

"If you're so good at reading body language, what am I saying now?" She glanced up with soft, longing eyes.

"Hum, you're sweating, so you body says you want to get out of these disguises as soon as possible and into my arms."

She laughed. "I guess you can read body language."

Starry commanded the guards at their door to leave. Then, giving the bound guards in their room a little more gas and memory wipe, they pulled them into the hall and left them there.

The overhead vid-screen came to life as the transport shuttle pulled away from the star cruiser. The news flashed on and who else did Starry see but Guard Jarrel being interviewed. He tapped Tramal on the shoulder and pointed at the screen.

"I hear you're getting a big promotion for this amazing piece of detective work." The reporter thrust the mic into Jarrel's face.

"Huh, yeah. Promotion, I'm being told."

"What evidence first tipped you off?"

"Huh, that's...classified. Sorry."

"Can you tell us anything about how you saved the fleet from certain annihilation?"

"Well, huh, it's all so fuzzy. Like some surreal dream. But I can say my mind is working all the time, even when I'm asleep. I get a lot done when I'm asleep." He stared at the floor. "Apparently."

"There you have it folks, people like him make heroism seem so easy. Back to you, Henry."

A beep from their wrist-vid interrupted their entertainment.

"Yes, Sir. Starry and Tramal here." Starry held up his hand so Tramal could see.

"Congratulations." Dolan's face focused on the screen. "You not only kept the *Armageddon* from blowing up, but found out the source of the problem. We're testing everyone, including myself, for the presence of Delirium and counter-acting it if found. All the students at the Academy who had been drugged had one teacher in common. Professor Quin. Evidence uncovered in his quarters links the Professor to the rebels. He masterminded this whole operation. We owe you two a big debt."

"Cool, we can retire." Starry showed his best poker face.

"Who said anything about money. We'll pay you with excessive praise. Your wage will remain the same."

"That's gratitude for you." Starry frowned.

Dolan smiled. "I thought the son of space-hippies wouldn't be so hung up on money. All you need is love, right?"

"Love, yes. Love for Tramal. Love for food. Love for gadgets. Yes, gotta have love."

Tramal broke in. "Yep, all you need is love, doesn't say what you love though, does it." She laughed

"And a little Delirium of my own would be nice too." He grinned at Tramal. Her laughing died off.

Monkey Madness

I told headquarters their idea proved they had developed a case of monkey madness. Never give a monkey a man's job. But did they listen? No. They trained and installed monkeys through the whole fleet. And now I'm sitting up in bed, a monkey holding a ray gun to my head.

"We're taking over the ship," the leader signed to me. "You've been holding out on us, and we want our due." He bared his teeth. "Are you going to hand it over willingly, or shall we take it by force, 'Captain'?"

I signed back, "How about a third option? You would get a lot further if you simply did your jobs."

Hoots and howls arose among the group of monkeys filling my quarters. The leader stayed focused on me and smiled one of those cheesy monkey grins I'd seen on old TV shows. "We put up with those jobs so we could take over. Stupid humans didn't see this coming." He raised his head upward in a victory howl.

"Yeah, I guess you're right, you pulled one over on us." Actually I hadn't been totally blind to the possibility. "I'll need to give the order."

He swung his limp hand at the com panel. "Remember, we have a ray gun trained on you. One false word..."

I paged the kitchen. "Release the bananas."

"Aye, Sir," crackled back over the com.

"Truth be told, I have a few in my quarters." I pointed at a locked storage door.

He nodded and jumped up and down. I opened the door and passed the bananas out. Hoots and monkey calls rang through the room. Soon they crammed the well-preserved yellow delicacies into their mouths. Smacking noise vibrated through the room. Ten seconds ticked by before they all dropped dead in quick succession.

Food remains one of the most powerful weapons. In this case, the poisoned banana.

A call rang through the com. "Engineering, Sir. The monkeys are all dead, but we have a problem."

"Yes?"

"The navigation controls have been set to fly us into the nearest star."

"Unset it then." I felt impatient despite myself.

"Can't. The master controls are in a room so small, only a monkey could access them. We would have to tear through the anti-matter bulkheads to override and change course."

I pounded my fist on the desk. Blasted moneys! I told headquarters the idea reeked. Especially monkeys designing ships, much less operating them. They've made monkeys of us all.

Space Talk

My foot is stuck! After all the years of space walks, I come out to fix a simple transmitter on this ship. What happens? I'm trapped on a ship half way between Neptune and Pluto!

"Bob, can you hear me?" Why doesn't he answer? Doesn't he know I'm in trouble? You would think a guy on a space walk would have a little help.

Don't panic. There has to be a way out of this short of cutting my foot off. Better check my air. Only five minutes left! Okay, focus, think, think, think....

Pry the boot out? Maybe with this wrench. Not a lot of leverage but maybe enough. That seemed to move it some. Ouch! No! It slipped! I've just added a wrench to the Kuiper belt! Darn, now what?

Three minutes left. "Bob, help me out here, I'm going to die!" Is this radio broke? Is he not responding on purpose? I know he is mad at me...but would he take it this far?

What? Is it alive? Looks like a bug, a wormish bug. Landed right on my helmet. What is a bug doing in space? How does it breathe? How did it hit my helmet and not become a splat on my visor?

What is it up to? No, not that! Can't let it bore a hole in my visor. Shoo fly shoo! Go away!

"Bob, I don't have long, I need air!"

Oh no! He's in! My air! It's escaping! What can I do? I don't see a way out of this. I'm doomed! Death by suffocation. Can it get much worse? No, don't say that.

Look, dots in space. Why, they're getting bigger. Oh no, that's me! I'm losing air. Feeling a little dizzy. Lungs aren't getting enough. Starting to collapse. Can hardly see...now. Probably....black...out....

Ouch! What...was...that? It feels...it feels..like..the bug is eating its way into my head. Is that what this bug does? Kills space walkers by removing their air and then feasting on their flesh? How insidious.

What a stupid way to die. Foot stuck, bug in my head, no air. I'll go down in space history as the first person to be suffocated and devoured by a bugonaut. Feast up guy! At least someone will enjoy this.

Why am I still aware? I should be dead by now. My lungs…I'm feeling air in them again. But how? Why? No air in my suit. My tank is out. How can this be? My sight is returning.

My neck… it feels odd. What did that bug do to me? I can breathe, but not well. I feel like I have a bag over my head. I do have a helmet on.

Could it be? Did that bug enable me to breathe solar air? Is there such a thing? One way to find out. Let's take this helmet off. It isn't doing me any good.

Oh! That is much, much better! Oh yes, I can breathe freely. I'm breathing sunlight in space! Must have been that bug. Must be a symbiotic being that needs me to survive. Did it sense I was in trouble? Is it intelligent life?

"Yes, I am."

Who said that?

"Your bugonaut, as you called me."

The bug in my head?

"I'm not really a bug."

I'm breathing sunlight and talking to a space bug in my head! I must be going crazy. This must be a dream. I'm going to wake up soon and have a great story for Bob.

"If you say so. You were dying and I saved your life. You tried to squish me but I helped anyway."

I'm stuck on this ship.

"What about 'thank you?' Do you only care about yourself?"

I can't move.

"Just get out of the suit."

Of course, I don't need it now. Yes! I'm free! Look! I can move around where I want! Cool!

What kind of bug are you now?

"I'm not a bug, I am a Delusian. I would prefer if you addressed me properly, after all, I did save your life and give you these powers."

Powers? I have powers?

"Well duh! You're breathing aren't you?"

Real powers? Like Superman?

"Who? Isn't breathing and moving around in space freely power enough?"

Can I lift heavy things, use x-ray vision, go through walls, turn invisible or something?

"Are you always this ungrateful? If you had such powers, what would you do with them?"

I would become a god! I would create races of beings, paint the sun different colors, reshape some planets. I don't know, whatever hit my fancy I suppose. You are my ticket to ruling the universe!

"What idiot have I burrowed myself into this time! Remind me to never join with a human again, I should have left you to suffer."

But you can't, right? You have to stay here. You have to do my bidding like a genie in a bottle. Right? Hey, are you still there? No….no, don't leave. No, I'm too far away from the ship! I'm out here in space with no helmet and no air! You can't leave! No, not now, not..when…I……was………so………..clo………

"Steve? Are you there? Steve…..can you hear me? Are you all right?

"Maybe this radio is broke."

Ship to Ship Rumors

Moth Man Rides Again

High atop Lothum, a colony on Mars, a vast network of structures float in the upper dome, greeting the distant Sun even as they shadow the underbelly of hidden greed, corruption, and crime beneath the red planet's surface.

But wherever evil exists, there also exist those who oppose it, who provide hope in a dreary world, and this one was no exception. For in a specific oval structure at the top of the dome resided Jim, one of Lothum's wealthier citizens. Inheriting the proceeds of his departed father and mother's Martian Mining Company, Jim wanted to give back to this struggling society.

So he researched and studied. Late nights consumed his thoughts and equations, until at long last he uncovered the reality he'd sought after. The reality that would provide him the ability to defend the weak and give hope to the stricken. On that day was born...

Moth Man!

Sitting in a clear, wrap-around chair, Jim sipped a cup of Taruazu coffee, blended from the finest chemicals, and studied his newsfeed, holographically projected above the table. He peeked over at his teenage son preparing to down a sandwich. "You did wash your hands?"

Rick stopped in mid-bite before pulling the protein-enhanced meal out of his mouth. "Cosmic memory lapse. I forgot."

Jim sighed. "Crime fighting requires you to be--"

"In top physical shape. I know."

Jim held up a finger. "A good example."

He shrugged. "But it's just you and me."

Jim cracked a smile. "What is done in secret will be shouted from the dome tops, son."

Rick nodded as he slumped. "Of course. You're right." He put the sandwich down. "I'll go wash my hands."

No sooner had Rick done so when the special bands around both their wrists blinked a bright red. Rick's eyes widened.

Jim turned the newsfeed off. "It's the Commissioner. Quick, Rick, to the Moth Hole."

They both leaped from their seats and sped to a row of bookcases. They stood in front of one, facing out. Jim raised a hand to his wrist band, but stopped when the study door burst open.

Jim's wife, Rocha, dressed in red slacks and a green halter-top, leaned against the wall. "Honey, the sink is leaking again."

Jim frowned. "Dear, can't you get a plumber?"

"I tried, but they're all tied up in the lower quadrant. It's just a drain connection. Can't you run to the colony supply depot and pick one up for me?"

Jim's mouth twitched. "Of course, dear. I'd be glad to."

She smiled. "Thank you." She froze and pointed at them. "Your alarms are going off. Shouldn't you be going somewhere?"

Jim and Rick glanced at each other. Jim cleared his throat. "Yes. It is time for...for our daily workout. Come, Rick. We shouldn't keep the trainer waiting."

Rick slapped his hands together. "Of course, the trainer."

They proceeded to head to the far door, but once Rocha had left and closed the door behind her, the pair halted and raced back to the book case.

"Warts, Dad. Isn't it bad to lie to Mom like that?"

Jim paused as he stared at the ceiling. "It is hard, but in this case, a necessary evil. The less she knows of our alter-egos, the less chance of hurting her. Besides..." He met Rick's eyes. "She would worry."

Rick nodded as he pressed his palms together before his face.

Jim's eyes focused before him. "Now, quick. There's no telling what evil awaits our attention. We must not delay." He pressed the button on the wrist band.

The bookcase revolved, pulling them into the wall, and replacing the shelving with an identical set of books. But as the pair spun into the wall, they traveled through a dimensional rift, empowering them with winged strength, and spitting them out into a cave buried deep inside an asteroid several thousand kilometers away from the Martian planet.

The rock wall turned and revealed the two crime-fighters: Moth Man and Firefly. Moth Man leaped from the perch, glided to the floor with his striped moth-wings, and then fluttered to a stop before a plain,

---

white table matching his white tights and silvery belt laden with pockets and gadgets. His eyes peered from a striped cowl.

Firefly buzzed behind him, his red suit blending with his yellow belt and tights and eye mask.

Moth Man waved a hand over the table, and a holographic vid of the Commissioner appeared before them. "Yes, Commissioner, what can we do for you?"

"Oh, thank goodness. I was afraid you were asleep." His gray hair cascaded over a wrinkled face.

"We are human, Commissioner, but I can assure you, sleep will not stand in the way of combating evil when it rears its ugly head."

"Well said, Moth Man."

"Now, what's the problem?"

"Oh yes." He leaned over and a screen flashed the image of a space vessel—a giant, black block fitted with fins on one edge. "I'm afraid the *Gallant* has been hijacked shortly after leaving port from our fair colony."

Firefly slapped his hands together. "*Gallant*, isn't that—"

"Yes, Firefly." Moth Man nodded. "The prototype ship that can induce hyper-sleep over the whole ship if necessary, or any one person selectively."

The Commissioner sat against a desk. "Exactly right, Moth Man."

"And do you have any leads on who might have instigated this treachery?"

The Commissioner nodded. "There is one person on the ship's manifest who could have done this."

Moth Man held up a palm. "Say no more, Commissioner. There is only one criminal mastermind who could have gone through security weapon-free and still pulled off a hijack like this."

Firefly slapped his hands together. "Cosmic telephone game! Rumor!"

Moth Man cracked a smile as he held two index fingers against the tip of his nose. "You took the words right out of my mouth."

The Commissioner's eyes widened. "Goodness! You're both right."

Firefly stood straighter. "Washing your hands does help."

Moth Man ignored the Commissioner's wrinkled forehead. "But never mind that, Commissioner. Where was the last known location of the *Gallant*?"

He leaned over to stare at his desk. "Sector 5.5, 6.3, about two hours ago."

"And you waited two hours to call us, Commissioner?"

He jumped off his desk. "Oh no, Moth Man. It was only ten minutes ago that we received the news ourselves—a transmission from the ship's captain."

"Can we listen to it?"

"If you think it would be helpful, yes."

Moth Man dropped his hands to his side. "Commissioner, to defeat evil no stone must be left unturned."

"Of course." He moved next to the vid screen and flipped a switch. Static flared across it before the screen revealed a man's head, with a ray gun barrel pointed at it. Worry had eaten into his captain's stoic facade, no doubt cracked by Rumor's relentless half-truths.

The gun jabbed against his head, jarring it to the side before he spoke. "Rumor has it our ship is on a pleasure cruise to the dark side of the Moon. Meet me there with bank account information to avoid alerting lunar authorities. You'll receive ten thousand creds for transferring the three million creds to your bank account." The vid screen returned to static before the Commissioner turned it off.

The Commissioner settled back down on the edge of the desk. "What do you make of it, Moth Man?"

Moth Man rubbed his chin while Firefly rubbed his gloved hands together. Moth Man held up a finger. "It is clearly a scam, a trap." He tapped his forehead. "Firefly, what rhymes with Moon?"

Firefly stared into space. "Loon, June, spoon, tune..." Firefly slapped his hands together. "Dune! Of course, the Martian singing group, the Black Dunes!"

"Yes. And what was the last rumor going around about them?"

Firefly paused for a second before jerking his hand up. "That they had died in a landing mishap on Io."

"Exactly. But they didn't die. It was a ship next to theirs that exploded. They missed their next gig due to the port shutdown, but they were quite healthy and alive. And where are they playing this weekend?"

Firefly's eyes lit up. "On the dark side of Mercury! That's where we'll find the ship."

Moth Man smiled and nodded his head. "That's the only possible conclusion."

The Commissioner's jaw dropped open. "How do you do it?"

Moth Man raised a finger. "If we were to tell you, we'd be writing the last page of our story. You wouldn't want that, now would you, Commissioner."

"Of course not!"

Moth Man jerked around. "Thank you, Commissioner. We'll take it from here." He waved his hand over the table again and the hologram vanished. "Come, Firefly, we have a ship to recover. To the Moth Craft."

The pair dashed to a spaceship, shaped like a moth—white and displaying Moth Man's tiger-striped-wings trademark. They flew through the air and landed in the open cockpit. Their hands flipped switches as the space-tempered glass slid over them and sealed onto the vehicle's body.

"All systems check out. Ready for liftoff," Firefly reported over the building hum of the engines.

"Engaging." Moth Man shoved a lever up and the ship blasted fire underneath it, lifting it into the air. A red glow emanated from engines attached to the end of the wings, and the ship lurched forward and veered up into a tunnel. Lights flashed by them as they gained speed until they burst into open expanse of space; the virtual asteroid rock-wall wavered as they passed through.

"Coordinates entered for Mercury's current position. Ready for the Moth Light Drive." Firefly braced himself against the back of his seat.

"Time to nab ourselves a vicious Rumor." Moth Man pressed the button labeled, "Moth Light Drive."

Stars around them swirled into a spinning cyclone of light until nothing but whiteness could be seen. The two crime fighters held hands over their eyes as the brightness peaked and then slowed until the stars again regained their place in the blackness of space. Except now Mercury floated before them.

"Firefly, engage the Moth Ship Locator. I took the liberty before we left to have the computer transmit the *Gallant's* ID frequency and code into our ship's."

"But Moth Man, wouldn't Rumor have shut that signal down or changed it by now?"

"Yes, he would have. But what he isn't likely to know is all ships are hardwired with a lower-level signal and that code is not publicized. It is unlikely he would know it or be able to change it."

Firefly pressed a button and stared at the holographic map that popped into place over the panel. A small bright dot blinked over Mercury's surface. "Cosmic sore thumb. They're right were you said they'd be."

Moth Man cracked a smile. "Nothing anyone who ate their breakfast couldn't have deduced. Now, engage the Moth Cloak. They'll never know what hit them."

"Engaging." Firefly pressed two buttons simultaneously. A shimmering film spread out before them while the wings drew back until it had achieved worm mode. Then the film wrapped around the body of the Moth Craft. As it clung to the steel skin, the ship appeared to vanish from the stars.

The *Gallant* grew in the view screen. The fifteen-story block with wings, maintained a low and slow orbit over Mercury.

"Moth Man, how can they maintain such a slow orbit?"

"Are you behind in your current ship design studies?"

Firefly frowned. "Warts, Moth Man. I should have been reading those trade periodicals instead of working on that puzzle."

"Understandable. Puzzles are important for mental sharpness. Besides, all work and no play--"

"Makes Rick a dull boy." Firefly nodded.

"Makes Rick a stressed superhero."

Firefly smiled. "Of course, I should have known."

Moth Man raised a finger. "They designed the ship specifically to maintain position on the dark side of Mercury to avoid overheating from exposure to the Sun. Using an anti-gravity drive, they are able to match the speed of the planet's rotation in combination with the gravity level needed to remain in orbit."

"Cosmic circumference navigation!"

"Speaking of puzzles..." Moth Man pointed at the ship now swallowing their view port. "How would you go about getting aboard secretly?"

Firefly rubbed his chin. "We can't use any of the entrances. They'd be aware of us as soon as a hatch opened." He paused, then snapped his fingers. "The Moth Holer."

Moth Man nodded. "Yes. It is a recent addition to the ship. Using the dimensional shift, we're able to create a dimensional hole, enabling us to pass through the hull undetected. Prepare for landing. If my estimates are correct, and they always are, we should set down beneath the second level fin."

Firefly flipped a switch, and a steering wheel rose from the console. "Shifting to manual."

The Moth Craft slid up behind the fifteen-story ship, rolling over the back fins, skimming the surface of the ship, rising over an outcropping of bulkheads, until arriving under the back wing. The ship's thin legs extended and cushioned the Moth Craft's contact with the prototype's skin.

A tube rolled from the head of the ship until it banged against the Gallant's hull. It sucked on and locked into place. Inside the cabin, a tile slid aside, leaving a hole in the floor.

Moth Man pointed at the exit. "Drop down that hole, and you'll fall into a storage room."

Firefly glanced at the hole and back to Moth Man. "You sure this will work?"

"Don't my inventions always work?"

Firefly raised a finger and started to speak, but stopped. The he shrugged and unbuckled. He leaped into the hole, followed by Moth Man.

As Moth Man slid down the tube, he heard a loud "Ugh!" before smashing himself into Firefly's crumpled body, eliciting further cries of pain.

"Cosmic sardines, Moth Man. I've hit the hull and you've hit me. I thought you said it worked?"

Moth Man groaned. "I failed to activate the dimensional field. My bad."

A button clicked in the darkness and the pair dropped onto a pile of rotting food leftovers. The two superheroes climbed out of the mess.

Firefly held his nose. "I thought you said this was a storage room."

"I'm afraid the lettering on the blueprints was a bit small. I must have mixed them up. But cheer up, Old Bug. The garbage room will work just as well."

Firefly chuckled. "Better. The smell on us should knock them out."

Moth Man cracked the door open, peered out for a moment, then opened it all the way and slipped out. Firefly followed. The two tiptoed down the hallway until they reached an elevator shaft.

Moth Man lifted his wrist band and dialed in a frequency. Then placed it against the bulkhead before clicking a button. The doors slid open. A shaft dropped into darkness below and rose into darkness above.

Firefly shook his head. "Wouldn't it be easier to take the elevator?"

"That would give away our approach. The more surprise, the better. Shift to infrared vision."

Firefly nodded and followed Moth Man by pressing a button on the side of his mask; red lenses slid over their masks' eye holes. Then they both pulled their mini-grappling lines out, pointed them toward the top of the shaft, and fired. The lines buzzed as they extended out, until after a few seconds a dull thud echoed back down to them, and their lines stopped. They both yanked to ensure connection, then swung into the shaft.

The two walked themselves up the shaft wall as they pulled the rope. Several minutes passed as they climbed.

"How much further?" Firefly paused to catch his breath.

"By my estimates, another seven stories."

A shaft door slid open and a head popped into the shaft. He turned back into the hall. "It's alright, honey. It's Moth Man and Firefly."

"It's about time!" a nasally voice echoed back.

The man met the pair's eyes and smiled slightly. "I knew you wouldn't let us down. Makes a soul feel good knowing you two are on the ship."

Moth Man cracked a smile. "It's outstanding crewman like yourself that provide the motivation to be here."

"And that Rumor fellow."

"If it wasn't him, it would be some other nefarious villain."

"So true." Then he ducked back in and the doors shut.

"Warts, Moth Man. It's men like him that make me proud to do what I do."

He nodded. "Remember that next time you're tempted to throw in the virtual towel."

Firefly grunted. "Somehow that doesn't sound right." He shrugged and they began the climb again.

A rumbling noise vibrated up the shaft. Firefly paused. "Moth Man, sounds like an elevator is coming up."

"No cause for alarm, Old Bug. The elevator is right on schedule. Prepare for plan *leap frog*."

The noise grew. Firefly cupped one hand around his mouth. "Why do you call it leap frog?"

"Because, you have to act like a frog and leap."

"When?"

Moth Man glanced down. "Now!"

They both leaped as the top of the elevator pushed up on them. They crumbled onto the elevator as it sped upwards.

"Get ready for the next leap. We don't have much time." Moth Man adjusted his wrist band dial.

Firefly pushed himself into a crouched position. As the elevator approached a shaft door, Moth Man pushed a button and the doors slid open. "Now!"

As the elevator slowed, they both dived through the open doorway, hit the floor and somersaulted over and back onto their feet.

"I've been wondering what kept you," a voice sounded to the side.

They both jerked around to see Rumor, in a full yellow jumpsuit, dotted with small, red tongues. A red mask covered his face with an image of a tongue sliding down his nose.

Moth Man faced Rumor. "Give yourself up now, and I'll make sure they go easy on you."

Rumor laughed. "Talk about rumors. You've heard too many. It's you who should be asking me to go easy on you, Moth Man."

Moth Man shook his head. "Firefly, why is it they never learn?"

Firefly slapped his hands together. "Because, evil destroys one's judgment, not to mention their taste in clothing."

"Flattery will get you everywhere, boy." Rumor pushed a button and six men in red jumpsuits, marked as if they were giant, walking tongues, leaped from the elevator.

Rumor smiled. "Get them!"

The six tongues leaped toward the two superheroes. Fists swung through the air, meeting faces, stomachs and groins. The six staggered back, then regrouped, surrounding the duo, and closed in.

"Bike pedal and windmill, Firefly!"

Firefly put his back against Moth Man's, and they locked arms. Moth Man lifted Firefly into the air, and Firefly pumped his feet as fast as he could. Moth Man swung him around, as Firefly's feet connected with faces and necks, bashing the six goons to the floor.

Moth Man faced Rumor once again. "Now will you come along peaceably?"

One of the goons rose from the floor and grabbed a nearby pipe. He crept toward Moth Man as Rumor continued to talk.

"You see, Moth Man. Rumor has it that your days are done. Over. Kaput."

The man behind Moth Man raised his pipe into the air. Moth Man batted his wings around the man, and a cloud of dust enveloped the attacker. He collapsed, his weapon rattling against the floor. "Moth eyes do have their advantages."

Moth Man picked up the pipe. "Perfect."

Rumor groaned as he rolled his eyes to the ceiling. Then pulled two ray guns from his belt and blasted the two superheroes. Both of them fell backwards and landed with a thud.

Rumor blew the smoke from his barrels and twirled the guns back into their holsters. "Finally." He stepped down to the floor, but as he did, Moth Man rose back to his feet.

Rumor slammed his foot onto the floor. "Why can't you die?"

Moth Man rubbed his head. "Low-level body shielding." He glanced at Firefly, still laying on the floor, a hole burned into his chest. "It appears Firefly forgot to turn his on."

Rumor threw his hands up. "At least that's something!"

"Not so fast." Moth Man pulled a pill from a pouch on his belt. "I brought along a ray blast antidote."

"Antidote? For a ray blast? You've got to be kidding. I've heard rumors, but—"

Moth Man shoved a pill down Firefly's throat. "Sometimes, rumors do turn out to be true."

Firefly blinked his eyes open. "Cosmic head trip! What happened?"

Moth Man flipped a switch on Firefly's belt. "You forgot your shield and died."

"Is that all?" Firefly climbed to his feet.

Rumor put a palm to his forehead. "Is that all? You've got a freakin' hole in your chest."

"It's just a flesh wound. I've had worse."

Rumor threw up his hands. "This never ends." He pushed a button on his belt. A force field slid from the ceiling and met the floor, surrounding the two bugs.

Rumor turned his attention to a panel and pushed buttons. "Rumor has it Command has lost their prototype ship, along with two of their finest crime fighters, in an accidental engine overload." The whine of the engines grew louder and sharper.

Moth Man slammed his fist against the force field. "You fiend! Do you have no compassion for the men, women, and children who will die on this ship?"

Rumor grinned as he headed toward the elevator. "Rumor says I care. But it's just a rumor, so I hear." He laughed as he entered the elevator. "I'm heading out on a shuttle. Maybe we'll meet again in the next life. Sleep tight." The doors slid shut, leaving the pair with a growing engine whine.

"Warning," the computer sounded over the bridge. "Engine overload in five minutes." Gas floated down from the ceiling.

"It's the hypersleep gas." Moth Man rubbed his chin. "It will take full affect in ten minutes, but it can make us groggy before the ship blows."

Firefly paced the floor, what little of it there was. "Cosmic bug zapper, Moth Man. What can we do?"

Moth Man placed his fingertips on the field's surface. "If I can vibrate my wings at the right frequency to sync with the field's, I might short it out."

Moth Man closed his eyes as his wings hummed in the air.

"Warning." The computer voice had adopted a more concerned voice. "Four minutes until engine overheat and ship implosion. Advise abandoning ship."

Moth Man shook his head. "No good." He thought for a second. "You add your wings too. You can beat yours faster than mine."

Firefly nodded and yawned; he touched the force field and vibrated his wings into a blur. Seconds passed as the two concentrated.

"Warning!" The voice sounded like a drill sergeant. "I said move it, soldier! Go, go, go, go! You have three minutes left."

The two continued to buzz. Electrons crackled through the field. Then popping noises rang across the bridge as the field collapsed in a shower of sparks.

"Warning!" a new voice pleaded. "I beg of you, don't do this to me. You only have two minutes to get out. Please, please, leave before it is too late!"

"That will be barely enough time to reach our ship, Moth Man." Firefly headed toward the elevator shaft.

"We can't leave this ship's crew to die, Firefly." Moth Man sat before a console.

He nodded. "Of course. You're right." He gazed over Moth Man's shoulder. "But how can we stop it?"

"We can't."

"But...but, you said you'd reviewed everything about this ship."

Moth Man paused from his button punching to stare into the wall. "I fear I was interrupted right as I was to read the section on how to stop an overheating engine. I never got back to it."

Firefly slapped his forehead. "Then why didn't we run?"

"Let that be a lesson to you, Firefly. You can never be too prepared as a crime fighter."

"Warning, you idiots! What kind of nut jobs wait until the last minute before the ship blows to leave? Get the <bleep> off my bridge! Now!"

Firefly twisted his mouth. "What was that?"

Moth Man shook his head and resumed his button punching. "Word censors. To protect poor, innocent children who might happen to stumble upon this story. No telling what grave injustices could propagate over their lifespans upon the chance hearing of one naughty word."

"Warts, Moth Man. You're right. I didn't think of that."

"It's also the reason you can only say 'warts.'"

Firefly raised an eyebrow. "Warts, warts, warts, warts. Hey, you're right. No matter what I say, only warts comes out."

"We all have our faults, Firefly." Two more beeps and Moth Man sat back in his chair. "That should do it."

The computer started a countdown in a voice growing in intensity. "Ten. Nine. Eight."

"What should do it?" Firefly stared at the console.

"Simple, really."

"Seven. Six. Five."

Moth Man pointed at numbers on the display. "I couldn't shut down the engines, so to keep them from overheating..."

"Four. Three." The computer began weeping. "Please stop me!"

"I set the ship to accelerate to maximum speed to burn off the energy."

"Two."

Firefly slammed his fist on the console, hitting a big, red button. The ship lurched and accelerated. "You forgot to engage the engines."

"One."

Moth Man leaned back in his chair. "Even superheroes make mistakes."

"Point five."

"Let that be a lesson to you, Firefly. Always remain alert."

"Point twenty-five."

A long pause echoed across the bridge as the two waited either for an explosion or the all-clear.

The computer sighed. "Whew. That was close. All systems are operational."

Moth Man cracked a smile. "Another execution of justice fulfilled."

Firefly let out a breath he'd been holding. "Ah, not quite, Moth Man. Rumor's gotten away."

Moth Man raised a finger. "Now, that's just a rumor. The truth is, I suspected he would attempt to escape and instructed our ship to lock a tractor beam on any shuttles leaving the *Gallant*. He's effectively imprisoned out in a small space craft, where he will remain until we return to Lothum."

"Cosmic checkmate, Moth Man. How did you do it?"

"The best way to defeat Rumor is with the truth. Be who you are, and Rumor will take care of himself."

"There." Jim pulled himself from underneath the sink. "That should do it."

Rocha opened the faucet; water exited the nozzle. "Any leaking?"

Jim examined the pipes. "Nope. As good as new."

She leaned over and inspected it herself. "Maybe you should take up plumbing. I hear it makes good money. Not that you need it, of course. But at least you'd stay busy doing something important rather than lazying around here all day like some rich guy."

"But I am a rich guy."

"All the more reason to do some work from time to time. Like getting exercise. It's good for you."

Jim nodded. "I'll look into it."

Rocha grabbed her purse and headed to the door. "I'll be back in an hour."

"Where are you going?"

"Daily lady's bridge club. Usual social stuff. You know."

Jim rubbed his chin. "Have fun, rich girl."

She turned in the doorway. "Thanks, but think about it. I think you should do the plumbing thing." Then she disappeared.

Jim shook his head before noticing his band blinking red. "Never a moment's rest for this lazy, rich guy." He rushed to the study.

The Captain's Chair

On a lonely space route, picking up strangers often promised a welcome relief from the robotic voices of the ship. Often the strangers grew into friends. Between hands of poker and beer, or the occasional game of Spaceopoly, I would learn about the strangest desires and the darkest secrets of my guests. Weeks with only a robot's voice for company caused a man to confess all given the chance. In my case, a woman.

But on occasion, I would take aboard the other type too. The one who wanted all you had, and often you as well. The dog-faced Lizowler happened to fall into the latter category. Many sought their wealth as pirates of the space lanes, and this one appeared to have done well for himself based upon the loot sewn onto his uniform.

He jabbed a coil-gun to the side of my head. "Ya have a nice ship here. I just might take a liken' to it." His jowls wagged as he talked while his eyes darted around and his nose sniffed the air.

I swallowed. Though I had successfully avoided death before, you could never know for sure how they would react. One second down the wrong path, and I would be space-garbage.

I stared him in the eye and presented my best helpless-female face. "You like my ship? You certainly don't expect a weak human to oppose a husky Lizowler like yourself?"

He straightened up. "Of course not. Especially the secondary gender of your race."

I swallowed again, but this time to keep down the pride that demanded to seek justice for such slander. My revenge would come later, if I twisted him the right way. Instead, I popped my right hip out while sliding my hand around the curve of my rear.

"I bet you'll be ecstatic that I am the secondary gender of my race before you're done with me." I drained my longing eyes into his twisted face.

"I've also heard humans are not to be trusted. Besides, you would make a poor substitute for a Lizowler partner."

"You'll never know unless you try."

He grimaced as if considering it, then growled. "You'll never know either, I'll make sure of that."

Inside, I smiled. Few pirates would trust a woman who wanted to give themselves to them. But a woman who cowered at the thought, they would gladly attack. Now, I needed one more step of pride by the hairy beast.

I pointed down the hall to a door. "If you're going to take over, I guess you'll be wanting the control room and the captain's chair."

His nose sniffed as if he could smell a trap. He waved the coil-gun. "You first."

Our steps clanked along the metal floor, backed up by the hum of the engine. Then, the echoing symphony climaxed with the clunks of the door-locks opening, and the squeaks of rusty hinges dying to a last gasp as it slid to a rest, then sounded a final cymbal-clash against the wall.

The control-room instruments provided the encore of beeps and whirs. Infinite space hung out the window as our earless audience. In the center, bolted to a stepped platform towering over the small area, a plush, high-backed, chair—no, not a chair, I'd say a throne—cast a commanding shadow upon an otherwise standard control center.

His eyes gulped in the sight. Hard not to, and I designed it with that thought in mind. Few pirates could resist the captain's chair. Never mind that a lone pilot could never reach the controls from such a lofty position. The jutting arms and purple upholstery claimed that anyone who sat therein would command the universe.

He stepped up, then spun his head toward me, ensuring his coil-gun remained fixed on my face. He reached the top and examined the commanding chair and its view, but continued to glance my way.

He waved his pistol at the chair. "Why do you have this giant chair?"

I shrugged. "I have a big ego. It suits me. But you should avoid the captain's chair, it doesn't suit you."

He faced the view of the stars and gently settled into the welcoming seat. One beep of an instrument passed before his scream barked across the bulkheads. The coil-gun clacked down the steps.

"What is this?" He yanked at his arm, then growled in pain.

I reached into a storage panel to retrieve my hand-ray. Then I strolled up the steps as he pushed forward, only to howl and collapse limp into the seat.

"I designed it myself, dog-face. Locking beams penetrate into your back and wrap around your spine, effectively immobilizing you. Any attempt to free yourself compresses the nerves and shoots jarring waves of agony across your body."

His eyes narrowed and he growled. "I knew you couldn't be trusted."

"*Au Contraire, mon capitaine.* You cannot trust your own arrogance."

"Now I suppose you'll have me as you wanted?" The edges of his mouth rose under his jowls.

I brushed my gun's barrel down his heaving chest, across his stomach smelling of alien sweat, and let it rest against his crotch.

"Na, I'm not in the mood anymore." I pulled the trigger.

I bounced the warm gun in my hand. "I really need to get a Disintegrator. These ray guns are too messy." Not that I didn't have a whole week before I would arrive in port. At least I could occupy myself with more than computer games that I had beaten several times over.

Maybe the next visitor would feel more like playing poker. Few could beat me at that game.

Father Jonah and the Renegade

Shashara strolled across the tarmac dotted with space ships of various sizes. Upon reaching hers, she stretched out her hand to unlock the door. From the corner of her eye, she noticed a figure moving among the shadows cast by the port's lights. She swung around, grabbed her fusion-ray pistole, and slammed the stranger against the hull of her ship.

She jabbed the gun against his head. "Who are you and what do you want?"

The rotating beacon flashed across her ship and revealed the grimacing face of a man. But his clothing—the black robes of a priest!

He forced a smile. "My name is Father Jonah, and I pray for a ride to Sardona."

She shook her head. He was a priest, and that didn't sit too well with her. She lowered her gun but kept a tight grip in case he tricked her. "I have to say, Father, I'm not the religious type."

"All the better."

She pushed him against the hull. "If this is an attempt to save a sinner, you can forget it."

He shook his head. "No, no. You don't understand. I need to get to Sardona as quick as possible. Lives depend on it."

Something didn't make sense. She released him, but kept the gun in her hand. "Lives? Look Father, I'm sure you're trying to do good and all, but I can't afford any charity trips."

"Didn't expect a donation. Would twelve-hundred Earthos be enough? That's three times the going rate."

Shashara froze. "Father, did you rob a bank lately? How did you get that money?"

His jaw set. "That's not important. Will you take me to Sardona in haste or not?"

She groaned inside. She didn't want to spend a week in space with a priest, but she did need the money. She had spent two and a half weeks on this filthy planet and couldn't wait to get back in space. Twelve-hundred Earthos would provide for another three months of expenses at least.

She returned to the hatch and punched in her code. "I'll probably regret this, but come on inside. We can discuss particulars."

He grabbed a couple bags from the ground and stepped into the ship, scanning the area as he did. Shashara had the distinct feeling she would regret this for more than religion. This priest would be trouble.

She patted the ship's pitch-black hull. "We'll make it for a while longer, Tet." She stepped in and closed the hatch.

Their boots clanked along the hallway. Unlike the outside of the ship, inside the metal shined despite bits of rust and dust. She led him into the control room. He slid into a wall-seat and buckled up. She sat in the pilot's chair and started the checklist to launch.

"Can any of your vid camera's see me here?" He craned his neck around.

"No. You're safe from prying eyes." Questions like these confirmed he hid something. "Father, you never said why or how you are saving lives on this planet. What's this mission about?"

He shifted in his seat and adjusted the belts. "Danger will pounce if you ask too many question." His eyes glanced up to meet her. "Spiritual, of course."

"If you say so, Father." He paid her well enough. Too much curiosity could lead to complications, and she didn't need complications. Ignorance in this business was more than bliss, it was security.

Shashara flipped a couple switches and the engines hummed to life. "Looks like we're a go. I'll radio control our flight plan."

"Hold on!" He twisted his mouth before speaking. "Tell them you're going to Telema and don't mention that I'm on board."

Shashara spun her chair around. "Father, who are you running from?"

He ran his fingers through his hair. "I won't be running much longer if you don't get moving! Please. Lives are at stake."

"I don't know, Father. You didn't include hazard pay."

"I gave you three times the going rate!"

She would have taken him anyway, but couldn't help milking him. "If they shoot down my ship, and I survive, I'll need a lot more to replace her."

He ground his teeth together. "All right then. I'll double it."

She nodded. "Deal." That would suffice for a down payment.

Shashara reached for the com switch, but an incoming signal broke in before she could engage it.

"Shashara, are you taking off?"

"Donar, good to hear you again. Yep, I need to get my space feet back, been here too long. Headed to Telema."

"Don't leave yet. You have a couple of visitors headed your way. I believe they want a ride. At least, that's what they said."

She met Father Jonah's eyes, and he shook his head. Sweat beaded on his forehead. She knew if he ran from someone, most likely from the System Confederation, these two visitors didn't care about rides. How did she get herself into these things?

"Sorry, Donar. Engines are charged for take-off, that energy's gotta go somewhere. Tell 'em to hitch a ride with someone else. Later." She cut the channel. "Here we go!"

She flipped two switches and the engines roared to life. The ship shook as it accelerated and Shashara felt the pressure of gravity pull her face down like putty being reshaped into a wide-mouth vase.

The all too familiar experience excited her. Like opening a present for Christmas, the anticipation of getting back into space often surpassed the pleasure once there. But if those visitors were SyCons, this could be a very short trip.

———

Father Jonah craned his neck to view the scanner. "Once we're outside Ungal's tracking system, change course to Sardona."

She frowned. "Father, I'm well aware how to do this."

He nodded. "Of course. I knew that. They said you could get me off Ungal."

"They?" Shashara frowned.

The com crackled. "Shashara, what's gotten into you?"

She sighed. Space control protocols went out the door when you knew the controller personally. "Nothing's gotten into me. I got into my ship and blasted off. What's so crazy about that?"

"It's not like you to pass up paying customers for a joy ride. They tell me if you return, they'll make it worth your while."

Shashara eyed Father Jonah. He stared back, his eyes pleading without saying a word. She twisted her mouth. "Who are these customers and what do they consider 'worth my while'?"

Seconds passed before the com came alive again. "They're rich folk headed to Telema, and they'll pay three thousand Earthos."

Shashara raised an eyebrow. The offer tempted her. Less risk and more money. It should be a simple decision.

Father Jonah leaned over. "If we go back, you'll be spending time in interrogation, and they'll give you no money."

She watched Father Jonah's face. It should be a simple decision. But could she trust him? He was a priest, or was he?

"Shashara, do you register?" Donar's voice broke the silence.

She sighed. A bird in the hand was better than two in the bush. Or was that a tree? She hit the com button. "Donar, too late. I've a date to make on Telema. I'll be late for it if I turn back now. We'll catch you later."

"If you say so. Fly safe."

"Thanks. The ship registered as Tet signs off." She closed the channel hoping the more official sign off would finalize the conversation.

Father Jonah let a breath he'd held escape. "Thank you. Those vacationers were anything but."

She swiveled her chair around. "Why don't you tell me who they were?"

His head sank. "It wouldn't be right to get you involved."

"Involved?" She flung her hands into the air. "I already know I'm probably carrying a fugitive from SyCon. Who knows what you're smuggling without my knowledge. If I had any sense I would take you back and hand you over."

He winked. "Then it's a good thing you don't have any sense."

She couldn't help but chuckle.

His smile faded. "Truth is, you aren't nearly involved as you think. Right now, you'll get interrogated and once they realize you know little, they'll eventually let you go." He shot a glance her way. "Of course, if you wish to sign on..."

She envisioned some monastic order or charity organization. Though why SyCon would be after him didn't fit. "No thanks, Father. I already have a job."

"As I suspected." He gazed out the view port. "Though we could use someone with your skills."

Shashara raised an eyebrow. "Are you really a priest?"

One corner of his mouth rose. "If I were, you wouldn't believe me. If I weren't, I wouldn't say so. You'll have to trust me."

She shook her head. "Great. I know nothing about you or why we're going to Sardona."

"Be happy that's all you know."

A beep grabbed Shashara's attention. She studied the scanner; a ship followed them. "Yep, here they come. As I expected."

"Can you do anything?"

"Of course. Let's hope they don't have stealth detection technology aboard their ship."

She flipped three switches and turned a dial. "Shifting to stealth mode." Lights dimmed to a low, red glow. "Transponder is off-line, and the ship's skin has rotated to its scanner absorbing side." She scanned a panel. "And engines are shut off."

She waited a moment before bumping the directional thrusters. By hitting them all on one side, it would send Tet on a different enough angle to avoid being followed.

She unstrapped herself and rose to her feet. "I'm going to get some food and get to sleep. In about four hours, we'll either be caught or we'll be able to change course to Sardona."

She stepped past Father Jonah, still strapped in. She paused and turned toward him. "Of course, you're welcome to join me at the table, if you wish."

He smiled. "I would. Thank you."

Blues and greens peeked from wisps of orange clouds on the planet below. Sardona had a reputation for being on the wild side, due to its location on the frontier of colonization. SyCon's influence in these parts garnered little support, which caused it to be a hideout for all sorts hiding from SyCon.

This destination fit the priest's escape from them. But what lives would he save on this forsaken rock? And how? And the biggest question: did she really want to know?

She twisted her mouth. Yes, she did want to know. Though she knew it would complicate things, she couldn't help but wonder and it would bug her for the rest of her life.

She caught Father Jonah's eyes as he sipped some coffee. "Father, are we free to land at a space port?"

He nodded and waved his hand. "Sure. I don't expect any problems here."

Shashara signaled planetary control as she established orbit. She pointed at the cup. "You'd better finish that. As soon as I have clearance, we'll be entering the atmosphere."

"Sure you're not up for a little baptism?" He winked.

She chuckled at the image. "Sorry Father, I like my baptism a little cooler."

"I can arrange that."

Shashara sighed and shook her head. "I'm sure you could." Like that would ever happen.

A signal beeped over the com. "Space Ship Tet, lock onto the Port Lomech signal and land at dock ten. Copy?"

She acknowledged the info, found the signal, and plotted the course. The firing thrusters braked the ship's speed and the altimeter registered their descent toward the planet.

The ship lurched as it hit the atmosphere. Father Jonah had finished the last slurp of his coffee and showed her the empty cup. "You're safe!"

Orange flames blasted over the ship, then gradually died off, revealing blue seas, green lands, and the orange clouds below. The ship's computers guided them to the space port, and they landed without a hitch.

As the engines whined into silence, She spun her chair around to face Father Jonah. "I've done what you asked. Do you have the money, or do I take you back to SyCon and hand you over?"

He feigned shock. "What, you don't trust a priest?" He winked and pulled his screen out from his cloak and handed it to her. "Here, plug in your account and I'll sign the Earthos over to you."

They plugged in their info, and Fr. Jonah showed her the confirmation screen. The money had transferred. "Satisfied?"

Shashara held up one finger, twirled around and plugged in the user name and password on the com feed to her account. Yes, the money had arrived. She smiled at him. "We're good to go. I guess you'll be heading your own way now."

He nodded. "Business to attend to."

She sat back in the chair and crossed her arms. "Are you really here to save anyone?"

He rose and proceeded to the door. "Oh yes. Definitely."

"Who? How?"

His head sank. "It's best if you don't know."

"And I'll go crazy if I don't know."

He shrugged. "That's probably better than the alternative."

Shashara rolled her eyes. "Fine. Have it your way. But while I'm here, I might as well head to the bar. I could celebrate, maybe find another job if I'm lucky."

He paused in the doorway, then turned his eyes back to hers. "Mind if I join you?"

She caught her breath for a moment. "Father, I thought you didn't drink?"

He shrugged. "Who said anything about drinking? Maybe I want to show my appreciation for getting me off Ungal."

"You've paid me well enough."

"True." He headed down the hallway. "You have a preference in bars here?"

Shashara smiled as she rose to follow him. "The Sinner's Loft."

"Great! Sounds like a needy place."

The pair swung open the bar's doors and entered.

"Hello, Father!" One man waved from a nearby table.

Others turned their head. "Hey, Father! Welcome back."

Several gave similar greetings as Shashara let her mouth fall open.

She settled into a chair at a table. "Father, these people know you!"

"They should. I've baptized and married most of their children."

A waitress approached the table. "Let me guess, Father. The usual?"

"Yes, and whatever my friend here would like, on my tab."

Shashara sat back in her chair and rubbed her forehead. "You have a tab here?"

"It's a figure of speech, since I own the place."

"Own the place!" She glanced at the waitress. "I'll need something strong. Like a bottle of whiskey."

"Whiskey it is." She swung around and headed toward the bar.

She twisted her mouth and leaned over the table. "You're not a priest, are you?"

He sat up straighter. "I most definitely am." He held his arm out. "Can you think of any other group who needs help more than those who visit bars?"

She shrugged. "Maybe, but it's so unconventional."

He smiled. "So was Jesus."

She raised a finger to scold Father Jonah for dragging Him into the picture, when two figures caught her eye entering the bar. She focused on them and caught her breath. "SyCons."

Father Jonah followed her gaze. "Stay put and act normal. Perhaps they aren't here after me. If they are, I've got friends here."

Shashara shook her head. "They won't know that." He could be right that they didn't follow him here, but how often do you see SyCons out here? More than likely they had managed to shoot a tracer onto her ship before liftoff.

The two soldiers scanned the room, and one's eyes locked onto Father Jonah. He waved the other to follow as he marched toward their table.

She glanced at Father Jonah. "I did my job. I have no reason to get mixed up in this."

He nodded. "You're only an acquaintance. But they may not buy it if they know I came in your ship. They'll interrogate you for a while, but you don't know enough to keep locked up."

Shashara nodded, but knew the "interrogation" would not be pleasant—not something anyone wanted to go through.

The two soldiers approached the table and drew their guns—standard issue SyCon Bolt 45s by their design. The taller one pointed his at Father Jonah. "You will both come with us. Don't try anything. More are outside ready to aid us."

Father Jonah smiled and met the man's eyes. "If you know what's good for you, you'll walk out of here. I'd hate to see you get hurt."

The man gritted his teeth. "Threats will only intensify your pain."

Father Jonah held up his hands. "Don't say I didn't warn you." He lifted himself from the chair.

The two soldiers slapped their necks simultaneously as thwarping sound hit Shashara's ears. Their hands landed on darts embedded in their jugular veins. Their eyes rolled up, and they collapsed onto the floor. A smiling bartender held a dart gun in each hand.

Father Jonah waved a thank you to him as he met Shashara's eyes. "Told you I had friends. They'll be out for an hour or two." He reached out a hand. "We need to get going."

She frowned. "I can walk out of here without so much as a glance."

He breathed deep as he stared at the door. "Sure, but they'll have guards around your ship. You can go through interrogation or come with me. I have a plan to get your ship freed and to make them give up their search for us."

She knew he was right. But could she trust him? What if his plan didn't work? Then she'd be implicated in knowingly aiding and abetting a fugitive from SyCon. Going through interrogation sounded the least painful way to get out of this. On the other hand, they wanted him pretty bad to follow him to the outer colonies.

"Shashara, the soldiers outside will be checking any moment. I have to leave now."

She gazed into his kindly face. "How do you know I won't turn you in?"

He smiled. "I'm hoping you do. Like I said, I have a plan." He glanced at the front door. "And if you want to know why and how I'm going to save a bunch of people, you'll only find out if you come with me." A twinkle shown in his eyes.

He had her. She had to find out. "All right, Father. I'm in." She grabbed his outstretched arm, and he lifted her out of the chair. She didn't like the thought of aiding SyCon anyway.

Shashara peered around the edge of the dock-tunnel. As expected, guards stood around her ship. But only two? They must not have brought a big crew. Since they had escaped out a back entrance, they didn't know if soldiers had stood outside the front door of the bar. SyCon tended to be overconfident.

"Are you good with your fists?" Father Jonah watched her eyes.

"Yes."

"They don't know your face. You can approach them without getting shot."

She grunted. "And once I do hit them, then I'll get shot."

He winked. "Let me deal with that."

She breathed deep, put a smile on, and strolled out of the tunnel.

As she approached her ship, the guards dropped their rifles down. "Halt. Is this your ship?"

She scanned the oblong, silvery hull. Viewport windows dotted its exterior while insect-like legs lifted it from the ground. It resembled an Earth June bug in shape. Tet had served her well, especially with the modifications she had added for stealth mode. The less SyCon knew about that, the better.

She shook her head. "Not mine."

"Then move along. You have no business here."

She smiled as she pulled her screen out. "Actually, I do. I'm a reporter for the local news feed. Naturally I'm curious why you're guarding this ship." She stepped closer. They would be reluctant to shoot her if they suspected she might be a reporter.

"Sorry, we can't answer your question."

She stopped inches short of their gunpoints. "Hum, let me see. I think you're harassing innocent civilians in an attempt to intimidate the local population." She wrote on her screen. "Why, I'll bet you're planning a massive take over of the planet too. Wow, that'll make big headlines. Thanks for the story!"

She turned and stepped away as if to leave.

"Wait!"

She smiled and turned back around. "Yes? Do you wish to change your story?"

They lowered their rifles. "What I can tell you is we are seeking a renegade from the law. We believe he arrived in this ship."

She stopped a couple feet from the guards as she wrote on her screen. "And do you have a name?"

"I've already—"

Their combadges beeped. "The suspects escaped. A girl is with him. Short, brown-red hair, medium build, wearing a blue blouse, and dark pants and vest."

Their eyes grew wide as they listened.

She dropped to the ground and swept her leg underneath theirs before they could react. They both fell backwards onto the blackened concrete.

Shashara jumped to her feet and threw herself onto the nearest guard. She allowed her knee to land on his chest, knocking his air out. She knocked his arms up and wrapped her fingers around his throat.

His face turned blue as he landed blows upon her cheeks. She felt blood dripping across her chin. His hits landed lighter and fewer until his eyes rolled up, and he slumped in her hands.

She spun around to find the other guard pointing his gun at her. "Hands where I can see them."

She kept her hands in the clear. Where was Father Jonah? She darted her eyes around hoping to see him doing something.

The guard nudged the rifle's nozzle toward her. "Where's the priest?"

"How should I know? He paid me to bring him here and we've parted ways." If Father Jonah didn't do something soon, she'd be going through interrogation and more for nearly killing a SyCon guard. What if his plan had been to ditch her?

The guard lifted his combadge to his mouth.

A black-robed figure emerged from the shadows behind the guard and slapped him on the side of the neck. The guard collapsed into a heap on the concrete.

Shashara breathed a sigh of relief. "Did you kill him?"

He opened his palm. A ring rested on his index finger; a thin point protruded from it about four millimeters. "Nope. Just put him to sleep for a while."

He scanned the ship's hull. "There." He pointed to the underside of the hull. "The tracer."

Shashara grabbed it and yanked, then kicked it, but it failed to move.

"You'll not free it that way. It's a magnetic code." He pulled out a cylinder and planted it over the tracer. He turned the rings on it to various points. On the last one, the tracer's lights changed from green to yellow and it fell into his hands.

She narrowed her eyes. "You aren't a priest. Surely not."

He chuckled. "Of course I am."

"How do you know the SyCon combination for their tracer?"

He sighed as he hit the hatch's switch. "I possess it without SyCon's blessings. It's part of what I can't tell you, nor do we have time right now. We need to get moving."

The doorway extended to the ground, and Father Jonah stepped upon them.

"Father, you're forgetting something." I pointed at his arms. "Do you intend to bring the tracer with us?"

He smiled and continued up the steps. "All part of the plan."

She shrugged and followed him in. She couldn't figure this guy out.

They'd launched without any further complications. But she knew as long as they held the tracer, SyCon would follow. Did Father intend to shoot it off into space to get the SyCons off their trail? She watched out the viewport as they rose through the clouds and the sky above them darkened.

"I'll need to take the helm now." Father Jonah leaned over the co-pilot's seat.

Heat rose to her face. "Like hell you will."

"That's where we'll be if I don't fly this ship—SyCon's hell."

Shashara banged her fist on the console. "You've seen me fly. You know I can escape them. Why would you do any better?"

He paused. "Because, we're not going into space, but back down to the planet. Where we need to go, I can't tell you. I know how to get there in my head. I have to do it."

She gritted her teeth. If she'd known the plan required handing her ship over to someone else, she'd gone through interrogation instead, without blinking. "I don't trust anyone with my ship."

He sighed. "Sorry." He swung his hand around to pat her on the shoulder.

Shashara thrust her hand out and caught his arm. A pointed ring rested on his index finger. She let out a shout and grabbed his neck, shoving him to the floor.

He wrapped his free arm around her neck and jerked her with him as he fell backwards. He twisted as they fell, and she landed on the ship's floor. She gasped as the air fled from her lungs, and pain raced up her spine. A fist landed on her face. A stinging numbness flashed across her head and blackness overtook her.

A throbbing head greeted her. She blinked her eyes to clear the fuzziness and attempted to lift her right hand to rub them, but ropes prevented its movement; they had been tied behind the back of her pilot's chair. She shifted her blurry vision to see the shape of Father Jonah sitting in the co-pilot's chair. She blinked a couple more times and she could see out the port. They raced along the ground between hills and mountains.

She grunted as she jerked against her bonds, but he had roped her firmly into the chair. "Let me out you backstabber!"

His kindly face glanced her way before focusing on keeping the ship between the mountain cliffs. "Sorry for knocking you out, but we didn't have time to argue or negotiate. SyCon isn't too far behind us as it is."

"I should have turned you in!" Every bone in her body cried to get her ship back. Options flowed through her mind. He'd have to let her out eventually. Then SyCon wouldn't be his only enemy.

He changed the con to a rarely used frequency, then slipped a device from his cloak, attached it to the audio input, and activated it. "Whale Rider to Donkey. Do you have your ears on?"

"You're not a priest! You're some kind of undercover agent. Like in those old vids."

He cracked a smile. "Let's just say, I'm more than a priest."

A voice echoed from the speakers, slightly distorted. Apparently the encryption device warped the signal.

"Donkey reading Whale Rider."

He spoke toward the audio input. "Coming in through port fifty-six in a Donley, class Xavier ship. Entry with debris in twenty seconds. I repeat, entry with debris in twenty seconds."

"Entry with debris, copy."

"See ya in a few, Donkey." He cut the comlink off and put the device back in his cloak.

They raced across an open valley toward a group of mountains. Tree tops rushed under them as the mountain grew large in the viewport. She watched the scanner and saw the blip representing the SyCon ship following about a minute behind them.

The side of the mountain raced toward them. She glanced at Father Jonah who focused intently on the landscape before him. Surely he would veer off soon. Instead, as the cliff neared, he increased the thrust and the ship shot toward the mountain side.

"Father, what are you doing!" In her mind, she calculated the point of no return before he could avoid the cliff face. About five seconds. Her eyes darted between the rocks now careening toward them and Father Jonah's focused face.

"You have to turn now, Father, or we'll crash!" A chill ran down her body when he didn't answer nor did he change course. Had he frozen in fear? She jerked as hard as she could against her bonds.

She screamed as the ship dived into the side of the mountain. She heard an explosion that quickly died away, leaving her screams echoing in total blackness. This was death?

"Will you please stop screaming. It's hard enough to concentrate."

The shock of hearing his voice jerked her back to reality. She slammed her mouth shut, embarrassed to have displayed such raw emotion. The hum of the ship's engines greeted her ears.

They hadn't crashed! "Why didn't you tell me?"

A glow appeared ahead. As they drew near, she could make out a series of light-rings extending through a tunnel. They flashed by and Father Jonah's bearded face showed a smile.

He glanced at her. "Would you have believed me and flown the ship into the side of a mountain?"

She twisted her mouth. "No."

He chuckled. "I didn't think so. I didn't believe them first time either."

"I thought I was dead."

"Nothing like facing death to cause you to realize what's important. Eh?"

The lights flashing by created a hypnotic effect. "But the explosion I heard?"

"Triggered by our entrance, along with adequate debris based on the ship type. To SyCon, it will appear we've crashed into the side of the mountain. They'll assume we're dead. The port creates an opening through a mile of rock, much like Moses parting the Red Sea. They can dig for days and not find this tunnel."

A knot formed in my stomach. "But the tracer?"

"I put it in the garbage chute while you were out. Ejected it seconds before we 'hit' the mountain. It's lying among the debris."

"Appears you had this all figured out. Sorry for going ballistic on you. But I'm still not very happy at having my ship taken over by force."

He winked. "Apology accepted."

The end of the tunnel approached. They entered a cavern illuminated by lights lining the ceiling. A series of squared buildings, adobe-like in structure, hugged the walls. In the center a modest space port housed several ships and a tower.

Father landed Tet onto an open dock. As the engine's hum died off, he swiveled around. "I do have to warn you, even what you've seen so far means you are one of us now. It's possible we could remove the last few seconds of these memories and leave you outside in the wreckage. You'll figure you somehow magically survived the crash.

"But once you leave this ship and learn what we're about, you're with us for good." He focused on her eyes as if seeking an honest answer.

"And if I escape and leave?"

"Then, as the one bringing you here, it would be my sworn and unpleasant task to hunt you down and bring you back. You'd likely be thrown in a cell.

"That's why I'm giving you this choice, while you can still make one. But if you chose to join us, then you'll find out why I'm running from SyCon and how you've helped me to save millions."

She thought for a second. "You know what you're asking, don't you? You want me to agree to join something with a no-going-back guarantee when I don't have a clue what it's about?"

He shrugged. "That's the nature of it. If I tell you what we're doing, then you've joined."

Shashara pulled forward, then realized she couldn't because of the ropes. "Huh, you don't suppose you could free me?"

He jumped up. "Oh, I'm sorry. Forgot all about it in the excitement." He paused as he grabbed a knot. "You've forgiven me for taking control of your ship, haven't you?"

She sighed. "Yes, I understand why you did it. I'm not happy about it, but we'd probably be in SyCon custody now if you hadn't."

He continued untying the knots. She knew this would be a life changing decision. What if this was a religious commune and Father lead it? But hidden away in the mountains? Who would go to all the expense and efforts to hide a religious commune down here? It's not like those are illegal.

She stared at Father Jonah's eyes watching her intently. Trust, that's what this all came down to. "Will I like it here? Be honest. You know I'm not a religious nut...no offense intended."

He chuckled and drew in a deep breath. "We take non-religious nuts too. I think you'll fit in nicely."

If she couldn't trust a priest, then who? She'd take the risk. "All right, Father. I'll join your...whatever it is."

He wrapped her in his arms and hugged. She squirmed for a moment, but gave up. The moment passed and he pulled back beaming.

She breathed deep. "First thing I want to know is what this trip was all about."

He sat down. "You were right. I worked undercover at SyCon. I am a priest, but our crew implanted a chip in my skull integrated into my sensory inputs. It recorded everything I've seen, felt, smelled, and heard for the last six months.

"My primary mission was to record the data on the Underground Rebellion on file with SyCon, then pervert or destroy it. SyCon chased me because they wanted the info in my head and to bring me to justice. If they obtained the data, not only would those in the Rebellion be at risk of attack, but we'd lose our cause to their dictatorial government."

She shifted forward. "Underground Rebellion? I've not heard of it."

"Not many have. SyCon doesn't like anyone to know there's a group out there succeeding against them. It works to our advantage in a way. The general population isn't looking for us either."

She shrugged. "I don't care for SyCon, but what have they done to justify a whole movement against them?"

He stared at the activity among the docks. "Have you ever read the book, *1984*?"

"Nope. Is that a year?"

He nodded. "Not when it was written, though. Back then, 1984 was far into the future, when a big government would control every aspect of people's lives and watch over them constantly to ensure compliance."

She scratched her head. "Okay, but what does that have to do with SyCon? They aren't controlling everything."

"No, but they're headed toward it, and if not for the Underground Rebellion, they might already be there."

"How? Give me an example."

"A prime example is religious freedom."

She groaned. Maybe she'd jumped the gun saying she's join. "How did I know it would come to religion!"

He waved his hands. "No, you don't understand. SyCon controls what people believe."

This should be good. "How? Shoot anyone who disagrees with them?"

He nodded. "Pretty much. You don't read about or hear about it. But if anyone disagrees with the party line, they disappear without a trace and are never seen again."

She threw up her hands. "But SyCon doesn't have a religion?"

"Sure they do. It's the religion of no religion. They equally squelch any religion that teaches more than simple morals. You wouldn't have noticed it because you aren't religious."

She twisted her mouth. "Then why should I fight to have it?"

He sat up straighter. "You're not fighting for religion, but for the right to believe and worship as you wish. Once a government gains control over what people believe, they gain control over the people. Every major dictator through history, both on Earth and since moving into space, shuts down all opposition, all opposing points of view, and only allows one side to be heard—their side."

The picture gelled in her mind. SyCon's belief happened to be hers. But she indeed had heard little other than negatives about any other belief system, as if ditching all religions was the sole solution. She did recall something of that in history classes.

He pointed to the people working outside the ship. "We're trying to do something about it. Not force people to believe a certain way, but to establish real freedom."

If what he said proved true, she would happily support such a cause. If it proved false, however, she could ensure this movement's demise from the inside. SyCon would reward her richly. It was a win-win for her either way. Shashara rose from her chair. "Then I suppose we'd better get started."

Father Jonah smiled. "Great! First, I'll introduce you to the crew. You'll need to get settled into your new quarters, and..."

He continued on as Shashara followed him down the hallway and out her ship's hatch. The busy people stopped to wave at Father Jonah, and strangely enough, at her too. She waved back.

A bounce in her steps confirmed that life had changed—for the better. Now being a renegade had meaning beyond herself. Something she could even...believe in.

The Cold Truth

Neil gazed at the blue planet's horizon displayed on the viewer. Many years ago, another Neil had placed the first human foot on earth's moon. Now history would record another first by a Neil: entering the atmosphere of the ice-giant Neptune. The ironies of history.

"Neil, are you listening, buddy?"

Neil's dreams vanished. "Uh, what?"

"I said, have we matched the wind speed yet? Focus, man."

Neil glanced at the ship's speed. "Uh, yes, we've slowed to match Neptune's wind speeds. We're ready to enter."

"Adjusting gravity drive to descend—" Simon pushed a button. "Now."

Neil felt the push of inertia as the ship moved out of orbit. The upper clouds of helium and hydrogen tinted with methane grew in the viewer. A jolt, almost knocking Neil from his seat, reminded him to buckle up. The fastest winds in the solar system bounced the ship around; they reminded Neil of the rapids back home. The ship sank into the current. Soon, the heat of entry gave way to ice crystals. The viewer blurred.

"Neil, you haven't turned on the external heaters yet. You want us to drop out of the sky like a lead ball?" Simon frowned with narrow eyes.

"Sorry, I don't know what's come over me." Neil pushed a series of buttons. "External heaters, on. Stabilizing wings, extended."

"Glad I haven't eaten recently," Simon said. He smiled, head bobbing with the ship. He leaned back in his chair but leaned forward again, and stared wide-eyed at the viewer as the ice-crystals melted.

Neil's attention froze on the viewer. The ship had broken into clear sky. The blue and white clouds rose as a ceiling over them. Clear air dropped for several kilometers to a swirling and raging ocean of liquid. A luminous blue radiated through the ocean and into the atmosphere as if a little star existed at the planet's core. Perhaps it did.

Neil glanced at Simon. "None of the readings said this was here."

Simon hit a button. "*Neptune 2*, come in. Can you read us?" Crackling static answered their hail.

"Now we know why the probes never responded once they entered Neptune's atmosphere," Neil said. "The gas-cloud covering the planet blocks radio signals."

"And radar, and all other wave lengths as well, at least the ones we know of." Simon peered over the horizon. "Might as well get busy with the test. Daylight's a burnin', as they use to say."

"Daylight? This is planet-light, eternal day." Neil turned on the cameras and initiated the first scan.

Neil read his display again. No, it couldn't be. Not here of all places. "Uh, Simon, take a look at these readings."

Simon stretched his body to see Neil's display. His eyes widened, "That can't be right. Must be something wrong with the instruments."

"What, pray tell, cannot be right?" said a voice from behind them. "That life exists on this planet?"

Neil spun around at the sound of the strange voice. Before them stood a blue creature. He appeared male, but not quite human either. "Who are you and how did you get aboard our ship?"

"Interesting, you invade my planet and you request me to explain my presence?" A smirky smile creased his thin lips. "Rather, I should demand a like explanation from you."

"Hold on," Simon said, "if you're from this planet, how come you can speak English? This has to be someone's idea of a practical joke. I'll bet Peter's behind this."

Laughter erupted from the blue being. "Truth is, I lived upon Earth, long ago. Then in 1846, the Saint Petersburg Academy of Science landed upon the name of *Neptune* for this planet. Naturally, the appellation commanded my attention, so I traveled here and discovered all seas and no land, which was greatly to my liking. No competition."

"What do you mean, 'naturally' it commanded your attention?" Neil feared the answer.

"Is it not apparent? I am Neptune, god of the sea."

"Yeah, and I'm Zeus," Simon said.

The blue being scrunched his brow. "My, you have changed since our last meeting."

"Ah, Neptune," Neil cleared his throat. "If you really are from here, are my readings correct? Is there life on this planet?"

He laughed. "Am I not alive?"

"No, I mean other life, indigenous to this planet. I'm reading the ocean is full of it."

"Oh yes, and much of it intelligent. But, avoid telling them I said that. I have taught a few English, but alas, few know it. Little use for it here."

"But how can life exist here," Simon said, "there's no oxygen here to breath, no land to live on, horrible winds and storms, and the pressure under that ocean must be thousands times greater than Earth's. What kind of life could exist here?"

Neptune shook his head. "Humans always have been prone to a restricted view. You believe life is only as you experience it. Life is much more persistent." Neptune stared out the viewer at the sea and pointed to a school of what appeared to be fish, breaking the surface and diving back under. "You have much to learn. It should prove entertaining to watch you make the attempt."

He then faded into nothingness within seconds.

They stared at each other in stunned silence for a few seconds and then back to the viewer. A creature broke the surface of the ocean and waved an appendage at them.

Neil turned to Simon and pointed at the viewer. "Did that creature just wave at us?"

"This has to be space sickness. Yep, has to be." Simon wiped his forehead.

Neil gazed out the viewer at the glowing ocean. "Or, it's another giant leap for mankind."

Weapons of War

"Target in sight, Captain," announced the lead ship as they dropped out of inner-space. A V-shaped line of one-seater, Shadowbird fighters flew in front. Captain Dan, in his roomier Rioter fighter, held the quarterback position.

Their target, a twenty-kilometer, cigar-shaped cruiser of the Kulugans, glowed with starlight against a colorless backdrop.

Dan's ship boasted a new weapon dubbed the *Acid Ray*. Metal-eating acid extracted from the *Caustic Nebula* would ride a shield penetrating plasma beam. Their cruiser wouldn't last an hour once hit. But, he had to fly within twenty-five meters to deliver the knockout punch.

"Sir, the Kulugan fighters have exited the cruiser's bay, but are holding position behind it."

"I'm smelling a trap." He gripped his flight stick tighter. "But what, I've no idea. Proceed as planned."

As they approached, the enemy cruiser emitted flashes along its port side. Waves rippled toward Dan's squadron, as if someone had thrown a rock into a pond. Dan realized too late that a strange new weapon raced toward them.

His heart skipped a beat. The greatest fear of man, the unknown, now raced at him. His last thought before impact: *One good secret weapon deserves another.*

Dan awoke. His head pounded. He forced himself to focus on the viewer through the pain—a gray screen stared back. He pushed the button for the view port to open—nothing.

Dan sighed. *Great, their weapon drained the power. Not a bad idea. Powerless targets make for easy prey. But, why am I still alive?*

Dan pulled a pole from an enclosure, which folded open to a crank. He struggled with the rarely used device; the view port doors ground open. He sat and scanned the spinning stars.

There they are. He saw rays shooting around a large ship off in the distance. *Surely one of them will break off to tow me back.* Yet no one came to his aid. The fight receded into the stars.

He checked his oxygen level, luckily a mechanical dial. He had enough for two hours, then it would be a slow, agonizing death.

After rolling through space for an hour, Dan arose and stared out the window. Rolling past the port, a cruiser emerged from the void.

That's the Kulugan cruiser? But, how can that be? Have I come upon another battle? A squadron of Shadowbird fighters in a V-shape approach formation with a Rioter ship behind them dropped out of inner-space. This had to be the same battle though it made no sense.

Dan figured the Kulugans would blast him. Yet, he drifted by the Kulugan cruiser, within the twenty-five meter range, ignored by everyone. He pulled the trigger, just in case. Nothing.

Dan saw his squadron approaching, except now he watched from a distance. The cruiser next to him flashed and the same rippling wave shot out toward the oncoming squadron. *Is this another wave of fighters? Or...* He didn't know if he should even think the thought.

As he watched, the wave reached the squadron and scattered the lead ships. As it hit the back ship, Dan's world went black.

Dan awoke. His head pounded. He forced himself to focus on the viewer through the pain—a gray screen stared back. He paused. *What happened?* He glanced at the oxygen meter, and it showed just over two hours of air.

He scratched his head. *So the rumors of their experimental, dimension weapon are true. By throwing ships into an interphasic shift, they lose their power. But it sent me too far in and now I'm stuck in a repeating loop and invisible to their eyes. That's why no one came after me.*

He arose, engaged the crank and opened the view port doors. As before, he watched a dwindling fight. An hour later, the fight came back into view. Again, he flew in close to the cruiser, it shot the wave at the oncoming fighters and when it hit the back ship, he blacked out, then awoke and rode the same ride.

He cycled through ten trips. Each time he studied the scene and planned his attempt to escape the dimensional trap. On the eleventh pass, he initiated his plan.

He locked his helmet into place and disconnected the oxygen tank from its fittings. Using the manual release, he opened the hatch. A rush of air flew into space. He anchored the tank on the hull with the outlet pointing outward. When the Kulugan cruiser rotated under him, he fired the makeshift thruster. Several blast of air later, he had adjusted course to collide with the Kulugan ship. Contact with an object should break him from the interphasic shift.

After closing the hatch, he attached the tank to his suit. The battle approached again. The cruiser filled the view port as he rotated around. He strapped himself into the chair and braced.

The two dimensions collided. Pops reverberated through the cabin like ripping bubble-wrap. Dan vibrated with his ship and everything warped like a flag whipping in the wind. As the sensation passed, he heard metal scraping as his ship rolled across the cruiser.

Power returned. With expert hands, he stabilized the rolling ship, spun it around, and fired the *Acid Ray*. A tightly focused beam tore through the shields and bored a hole into their ship. A glowing red infestation widened.

He fired thrusters to escape. Cheers rolled over the com. "Sir, how did you—"

"No time now, Sergeant, just turn your tail and run. Now!" They complied without another word. A wave shot from the cruiser, but it dissipated before it could reach the receding ships.

Dan scanned the cruiser; the hole enveloped a quarter of their ship. Mission accomplished. But at what cost? War has always been Hell, with no winners.

He peered into the view port of the ship next to him. His own face stared bug-eyed across the near vacuum at him.

"This won't be easy to explain to myself."

Spacy Date

Larry gazed at Rebbecca as she stared at the stars from the view port. "Sure you don't want to join us for the Christmas party?"

She didn't move. "No thanks."

He rubbed his chin. She'd volunteered for this expedition to the outer edge of the solar system, yet the whole time she'd paid minimal attention to her work and spent hours staring at the stars. Yet, she remained closed off to everyone.

He moved toward her. "Maybe it would help to talk about what's bothering you."

She met his eyes, her sandy-brown hair danced upon her shoulders. "No offense, but I'd rather not."

Larry stared out the port. His eyes caught sight of Pluto, which they had been following for a few days. Eventually they would catch up with it and set down to explore for a while.

He nodded out the window. "You looking for something?"

She frowned but refused to face him. "I'd rather be left alone. Please."

He sighed and walked away. "I hope you'll find a way to join us for the celebrations. Christmas is tomorrow, you know."

She remained frozen at the port and refused to answer.

He shrugged and headed for the door.

An annoying buzz crackled through the air and red lights flashed on the consoles. Larry jumped, and then hurried to the console. A second passed as he studied the readings.

Rebbecca watched over his shoulder. "Radiation is increasing."

He nodded. "Yes, but why? Remains of a solar flare?"

The captain pulled the door open and entered. "Report." Several crew members filed in behind him.

Larry stood at attention. "Sir, radiation is increasing. Cause, unknown. Investigating."

He rubbed his chin as he sat in his chair. "How long before it reaches critical?"

"At this rate, about five or ten minutes."

"Don't stand there then. Investigate!"

Larry whispered in Rebbecca's ear. "I'll need your help. And your full attention. Got it?"

She nodded and pulled her hair back.

"Trace the trajectory. See if you can discover where it came from."

She already had her hands on the controls, doing just that. "I'm on it."

While she worked on that, he struggled to find a solution. How wide and big did the radiation span? Could they fly out of it in time? He scanned the area to get an idea of its extent.

She jerked her head up. "It's coming from an asteroid not far away."

The captain leaned over in his chair. "Do you have a fix on it?"

"Yes, Sir."

He focused on Tom. "Get those coordinates and destroy that asteroid."

"Yes, Sir."

"No! Wait!" Rebbecca rushed toward the captain. "You can't do that!"

He frowned. "We have a few minutes to live if we don't. You'd better have a good reason and spit it out fast!"

"Well, I believe..." She stared at the floor. "...that its my husband."

The captain's mouth dropped open. Larry realized his had too. Silence prevailed in Control.

The captain blinked. "We don't have time to confirm what you just said, but even if its true, we'll all die if we don't take out that asteroid. I'm sorry." He nodded toward Tom to fire.

Five missiles blasted from their bays. Larry watched through the port as they landed on the rock drifting about a mile away, and it broke apart.

The captain fixed his eyes on Larry. "Report."

Larry checked the instruments. "Radiation is going down, Sir."

The captain slapped the chair and rose to his feet. "Good work, everyone. Now we can continue with the party."

The Control crew filed out behind him, leaving Rebbecca and Larry alone. He stared at her for a moment. Could that really have been her husband? How and why? Did she know something he didn't? Or had grief made her delusional?

Obviously the captain didn't think anything about it. But, even if it wasn't true, it was to her. He figured she would prefer to be alone, though he longed to comfort her in some way. He turned and headed toward the door.

"He's really dead."

He halted in mid-stride and spun around.

Her eyes turned to meet his. "He died last year, right before Christmas. His last words were, I'll meet you in the stars, out on the outer rim of the solar system."

She returned to staring out the window. "I knew he would be out here somewhere. He promised."

"And you think we just killed him again?"

"No, not killed. That already happened." She let out a long breath. "It's where I should have joined him on his journey into the stars. But now we're separated. Forever."

A chorus of laughter echoed through the metal walls and then a song rose to Larry's ears.

Peace in space and good will to all,
Christ is born in Bethlehem...

He smiled. "Maybe not, forever."

Justice in the Balance

Gil allowed a growl to roll from his throat. "I asked to see your departure manifest."

The bald man across the counter avoided eye contact. "I...I can't give you that information without authorization from TESA." The *Terran Expatriate Settlement Agency* seal glared at Gil from the back wall. Organization wasn't TESA's strong point.

Gil gritted his teeth as he reached across the counter, grabbed the man's ID scanner, and planted it on the back of his own neck. The attendant jumped, but his eyes froze as the scanner read Gil's chip and displayed his info on the holographic screen.

The man's bald chin dropped open. "You have top classification from TESA?"

Gil placed a hand on his gun. "Yes. Now give me the manifest. Or do I need to blast my way in to get it?"

"Oh no. Of course you can see it." He pulled the interface toward Gil and the holographic display swung into view.

Gil placed his palm on the interface pad and commanded the program to search for the name, "Jaya."

Nothing. Gil frowned. *What did Commander Rowl say the name of her ship was?* He thought for a second. "*Susan.*" He had chuckled at the debriefing hearing that; it sounded so plain. The search displayed the arrival and departure times for a ship called *Susan*.

He smiled. She'd left Trancor five hours ago. The flight path she filed would take her a good week to arrive at her destination. He'd be able to catch up with her, probably by the time she reached Sirus' orbit. He mentally recorded the info before shoving the interface back to the attendant.

"Thank you." Gil headed toward his ship.

"No problem...any time, sir."

Gil's thoughts returned to Jaya. When Commander Rowl told him what she'd done, his field of vision had narrowed as images of rubble and the stench of burning flesh invaded his thoughts. The events on Mars so many years ago had flashed before him.

Flames lapping at their house, his mother screaming, his father rushing the family to safety. He also held the memory of seeing his younger brother's charred remains before his mother pulled him away. His father had joined the posse to track the raiders down. He returned in a casket. They said the Raiders killed him.

"Inspector Gil," a voice broke through his thoughts as he reached to open his ship's hatch. Gil spun around and gritted his teeth. Before him stood Sergeant Drake, the man he'd beat out for TESA's Chief Investigator position.

"Yes, Sergeant."

"After another terrorist?" His lips curled sarcastically.

"It's not protocol to share mission data, Sergeant. Keep your nose to your own missions."

"Oh, I am, sir. I am." His eyes shifted to the sky. "But couldn't help overhearing you're after a ship named *Susan*."

Gil pulled within inches of the man's face. "Sergeant, you will stand down and leave this matter in my hands. Do you understand?" The gall of the backstabber to spy on him.

"Yes, sir. But I must report, sir, that we've been ordered from high command to stand ready to assist you. We've been assigned to the *Follet* patrolling this sector."

"Enjoy your vacation then. You'll get no call from me. I work alone."

Drake smiled. "Good. Makes my job easier." He swung around and walked off without so much as a salute.

Gil stalked toward him, but stopped. He looked into the sky. Jaya flew further away every minute. He didn't have time for playing arrogant games.

He entered his ship, the *Dracon*, sat in the pilot's seat, and focused on the controls before him. He checked through the pre-launch sequence automatically. After lifting off and breaking orbit into the starry blackness, he leaned back in his seat and stared into the abyss.

Commander Rowl had said she'd not only burned down a house on Athenia, she'd murdered its inhabitants, including two children.

He peered into the blackness looking for the first signs of her ship even though he knew it would be another twelve to fifteen hours before he'd catch up. But he could think of nothing else.

Gil dug into a book about a couple of guys running from a planetary version of the mafia in an attempt to forget about Jaya. It didn't work. The villain reminded him too much of her: bloodthirsty and unfeeling. She didn't care what havoc she rained down on people's lives, as long as her selfish goals were accomplished. She didn't care—

A beep from the console jerked him from his thoughts. His eyes settled on the spadar 3-D display. The readout indicated a Mark II ship. Its spadar range fell short of his own; she'd pick him up in a few more minutes. He watched as the ship ID info filled the screen. *Susan*, it read.

He smiled. *Got her!*

He sat up in his seat and watched as her ship grew on the screen. She hadn't bolted yet. Surely she'd spotted him by now. Unless she'd spent too long in the bathroom.

As he approached, her ship's thrusters fired, slowing the vessel to a stop. Gil sat back in his seat and rubbed his cheek. *What is she up to? Could this be easier than he'd expected?*

He set the controls to maneuver beside her. "It's either a gift or a Trojan horse."

Once beside her, he extended the docking lines. No sooner had he shot them out, when her engine flared to life, and she blasted away.

Gil slammed his fist onto the control panel. "Blasted Raider!" He clicked to retract the docking lines. A flash exploded from the screen and she disappeared into a hyperjump.

His fingers danced on the touch-screen, which responded with a series of beeps and purrs.

"You think you can escape from me, do you? I'm not shaken that easily." The trajectory of her jump locked into the navigational computer, his finger hovered over the firing button. A gnawing feeling caused him to pause. *Why? What have I missed?*

He sighed. *Better to get it right*. He initiated scans on the spadar. A minute ticked by but no heat signature nor echo of a registered ship. *Maybe she really had gone into hyperspace?*

Still... He tightened the resolution and adjusted its beam to register engine radiation. He focused the beam at a suspicious hole in the star field. *It's either dark matter or her ship.* The spadar beeped, and a blip appeared on the 3-D display.

His fingers slid across the pad and the computer drew the object's projected course through the floating images.

He leaned back in his chair and smiled. "She's heading to Sirus." He laid in a new flight path. "That little trick might have fooled a standard cop, but not me."

He decided to wait until she had flown out of range. She'd be careless and in less of a hurry if she thought she had lost him.

He frowned. Standard protocol demanded calling for backup when tracking someone onto a planet, and only the *Follet* could assist him. *Gil, you idiot. You had to open your big mouth with Drake.*

His own pride had put him into this situation. Now he'd have to swallow some humility. He sighed and signaled the *Follet*.

A crackle followed by a voice echoed over the speakers. "Sergeant Drake from the TESA ship, *Follet*, in."

Gil allowed his head to bump against the back of his seat. *Why him?* He straightened up to keep a confident tone.

"This is Inspector Gil of the TESA ship, *Dracon*."

"Inspector! I suppose you are calling to let us know you've caught the terrorist and would like an escort patrol for security?"

Gil grumbled. Drake's sarcastic tone galled him, making a difficult situation worse. "No, Sergeant. Per protocol, I am requesting backup to the planet Sirus. My target has escaped my initial attempt to capture her."

Drake's voice grew weaker as if he'd turned away from the com. "Hey, boys and girls. The vacation's over!"

Gil heard laughter in the background. No doubt they'd taken bets on whether he'd call or not. He felt his face flush, but forced himself to remain calm. He didn't want to give them the reward of knowing they were getting to him.

"Proceed to the planet Sirus. You'll receive further orders later. Over." He slapped the comlink off before Drake had a chance to sign off.

He shook the thoughts from his mind as he laid in a course for the planet. He refused to let them distract him from his job. Jaya would not escape him a second time.

Gil pushed aside the leaves of a bush as he entered a clearing. Her ship laid nestled among a group of trees. The vast number of caves in this region of Sirus created multiple hiding places. He smiled as he followed her trail. *She didn't count on a trained tracker pursuing her.*

Her trail led from the ship to a cave a short distance away. His scans for her ID chip proved useless. She must have removed it. Not smart. She would be quickly discovered at any planetary space port. He couldn't imagine how she'd avoided capture this long. He steeled himself for anything. *I will not underestimate her again.*

He worked his way to the cave's entrance and froze beside it, his back to the rocks. He slid out his baton, a force-field projecting device that could knock someone out if close enough, as well as provide a shield for him.

He checked his wristband; it picked up a faint ID signal. So she did have one, but not standard issue. The weak signal couldn't pinpoint her location, but it had to be her ID chip.

He twisted his mouth. He'd be most vulnerable as he entered the cavern. She could take him out as his eyes adjusted to the darkness. He peeked around the opening and spotted some boulders nestled against one wall of the cavern.

He slipped through the entrance and sped toward the boulders, his baton humming in one hand. He reached the rocks' protection and crouched behind them. He breathed easier; she hadn't fired. She either hadn't recognize him or had wandered too deep inside.

If she didn't know he followed her before, she did now. The noise of diving behind the rocks had lost any surprise advantage he had. Could he reason with her? If not, at least he could use her voice to zero in on her location. And it would give his eyes time to adjust.

"Jaya, I know you're in here. Why don't we talk this out? Why end up injuring or killing one another?"

Sounds of water dripping deep in the cavern answered him. He waited, hoping to hear some evidence of her movements. Nothing. He'd have to flush her out. His eyes now more attune to the darkness, he rose and slipped along the wall as quietly as possible.

Gil winced as his foot brushed against an outcropping of rock. Every sound echoed through the cavern. He might as well yell out, "Here I come!" *Why did I bring the night-vision glasses instead of the infrared ones? In a pitch-black cave, they're useless.*

He hoped she didn't have infrared glasses or he'd be a dead man in short order.

He paused and listened, the only sense that would help him now. A drip of water plunked in the distance. As its echoes faded away, his eyes widened. He thought he heard something, a slight shuffling noise as if someone had scooted their feet across rock. He focused and realized he could hear her breathing. It sounded as if she hovered right over him.

She's at the other end of this room—the acoustics allow me to hear her! That means she can hear me too.

He decided to take advantage of it. He let a low growl escape his throat as his hand felt along the ground. Finding a small rock, he threw it across the room to where he suspected she might be hiding.

The rock banged against stone. Its echoes joined the sound of someone jumping back and a barely audible exclamation.

Gil held still and waited. He hoped the pressure would build, causing her to take a chance and make a run for it. Seconds slipped by. One of them had to move first, and it wouldn't be him.

A blue light flickered in the distance against a wall. Gil smiled. *That's it, come to judgment day.* The light bounced up and down; Gil could see her form stepping quickly among the jagged cave floor.

Gil slid his gas pistol from its holster and slipped his breathing filter into his mouth, the nose cup snuggled securely in place. As she approached, he stepped from behind the stalagmite.

"Freeze, you're under arrest!"

She froze, but only for a second. She dove to the side and swung a gun out.

Gil dropped his aim to lead her and fired. She arched her back; the bullet shot under her. Gil heard the echo of escaping gas against rocks.

The dodge caused her to fall, firing a ray blast as she dropped to the floor. Gil ducked and rolled toward her, the blast shooting over his head.

Cracking noises preceded a loud rumble, shaking Gil's body. He turned to watch the entrance filling with cascading rocks, cutting off their only escape.

He slipped another gas bullet into his right hand as he threw himself toward the woman. He wrapped an arm around her neck. She kicked back under his grip. Welts formed on his side, but he pinned her head against a rock and smashed the plastic top of the gas bullet against the stone. Gas flooded her face. Her kicks lost their punch until she fell limp in his arms.

She'd wake up in an hour or two, but she'd be tied up, and Sergeant Drake's troop would dig them out. *Great, he'll never let me live this down.*

He shoved her to the side and lay on the ground. The blue light illuminated her narrow face and short red hair—if the blue light didn't trick his sight.

Gil smiled. *But no one can claim I didn't finish the job. Drake won't get the credit for this one.*

Gil rested for a moment before binding her arms with his plasticuffs. He wrapped her feet with a cord and tied it off to the cuffs. He pulled his wrist communicator to his mouth and relaxed. This would be fun.

"Inspector Gil calling Sergent Drake. Respond."

"Sergent Drake, in."

"I need further assistance."

The end of a chuckle started the transmission. "Did she leave you in need of rescuing, my friend? Maybe it would be easier if I went after her."

"Actually, I am in need of rescuing." He struggled to maintain a serious voice. "But I have the terrorist captive, laying right here beside me, out cold and cuffed."

A few seconds ticked by before the reply echoed in the cave. "Oh, I see. Well, what can I do for you?"

"Weapons fire caused a cave-in at the entrance. Lock onto my signal. I need you to dig me out."

"Sure, Inspector. Sergent Drake, out."

The tone of disappointment hung heavy on those last words. Gil allowed himself the luxury of laughing. No one could hear him anyway.

Gil heard movement; he turned his attention toward Jaya. She'd cracked her eyes open. Probably assessing her situation and planning her next move.

Gil activated the recorder on his wristband and jabbed her in the ribs with his boot. "Awake, are we?" He crouched down to get a better look at her face. "If you confess now, it will go easier on you. I'm recording."

Her jaw clinched, then she spit in his face. "Go easy on me? They left that option behind a long time ago."

Gil stood and wiped the spittle from his cheek. "Have it your way. The penalty for mass murder of a family will get you life. Confession might at least get you into a more pleasant facility."

She burst out laughing, which caused Gil to raise an eyebrow. Her mouth curled downward. "Try penalty for standing up to TESA. They killed my family. What do I care if I spend the rest of my life in some God-forsaken dungeon."

Thoughts flashed through Gil's mind. Images of the posse returning without his father, of his sister and mother lying in their caskets. "Tell me about it."

She wagged her head. "What do you care? This is just a paycheck to you. It's personal for me."

Gil clinched his fist. "Personal? You want personal? I'm out here hunting scum like you down because my family died at the rebel's hands. Killing innocent people is terrorism in my book. You bet it's personal!" His face felt hot. He had to keep his cool, remain professional. He didn't want to give her a legal loophole to freedom. Not now.

The harsh lines on her jaw softened. "I didn't kill anyone. TESA wanted my land. When I wouldn't sell, they killed my whole family, burned down the house, and then blamed me for it. I lost everything dear to me that day. I vowed I'd fight them until I died."

Gil sat on a rock. "You're copying my story."

She grunted. "I knew you wouldn't believe me. It's pointless."

"If you had proof of some kind..."

She bit her lip. He waited; she appeared lost in thought. A few moments passed, and then she met his eyes. "I do have proof, but it has to get to the right people. Not TESA, but Earth. They have to know what is going on here."

She's good. Gil scratched his chin. When his family had died, TESA had convinced him he didn't need the land, and he had sold it to them. He didn't care, he had only wanted to find his family's killers and bring them to justice. If what she had said was true, he had rewarded his family's killers instead. The possibility turned his gut.

He focused on her eyes. "If you have proof, I promise you'll stand trial on Earth. I'll see to it myself." It would be easy enough. He'd act like he was taking her in. By the time TESA realized he'd left for Earth, it'd be too late.

Jaya twisted her mouth for a few seconds. Then let out a breath. "Did you have trouble reading my ID chip?"

"Yes."

"That's because most of it is a sensory recording device. When on, it records in vid format what my eyes see and my ears hear." She paused. "I recorded the meeting I had with an officer named Rowl from TESA, right before my family was murdered by them. Go ahead, access it."

Gil moved his wristband close to her neck and punched the screen a couple times before he found the vid feed. The screen blackened a second before an office appeared. Behind a desk, Commander Rowl sat in a tall, black leather bound chair. But the man standing behind him and off to the right was none other than Sergeant Drake.

Commander Rowl leaned over his mahogany desk. "Let's not play games, Mrs. Jinkins. We need your land and are willing to pay for it. But this is your last offer."

"If so, I'm glad. I'm tired of these games as well. We don't want to sell. Our sweat has made a home here, and we aren't ready to give that up."

Rowl leaned back in his chair. "I would highly suggest you take this last offer."

"Or what? Kill me? Once such news reached the Terran authorities, they'd dissolve your corrupt butts."

He smiled. "Mrs. Jinkins, I'm afraid you greatly underestimate us and your situation." He leaned toward her again. "You do love your family, don't you?"

Her voice cracked ever so slightly. "Of course."

"We'd hate to have anything...unfortunate happen to them, now wouldn't we?" Commander Rowl shoved a contract toward her. "Sign now, and we'll make sure they remain safe and secure."

A moment passed before Jaya responded. "No, we will not sell."

Commander Rowl glanced at Sergeant Drake and nodded. Drake's eyes darted to Jaya, then he turned and left the scene.

Commander Rowl sat up. "I'm sorry we couldn't come to a mutual agreement. One sided agreements aren't nearly as...profitable. Good day, *Miss* Jinkins."

Gil shook his head. It certainly appeared to be Commander Rowl, and the appearance of Sergeant Drake lent credibility to the vid.

The scene changed to the interior of a land rover. Jaya's voice broke over the whining of the rotors failing to ignite. "My rover worked fine when I arrived, but now it won't start. I suspect Rowl is behind this." She released her thumb from the start panel and exited the vehicle. "Appears I'll have to walk home or catch a ride."

The vid faded to dark again, then screaming burst over the wristband, and the screen revealed a house burning, and bodies lying on the yard. "I...I never thought they'd go this far!" She broke down in sobs. The crackling of burning wood echoed before her as she ran into the yard. She knelt by a man, sandy hair stained with blood and dirt. Her eyes took in the twisted bodies of her children, one blackened by the fire.

"You bastards!" She screamed, and Gil thought she might die right there with them. Her face fell onto the body, sobbing. The vid went dark.

Jaya's wet eyes stared at Gil. "Are you going to hand me over to TESA?"

He barely heard her question. He slammed his fist upon a rock so that the physical pain matched his inner pain. Had TESA really been the ones to kill his family? Had he been working for the very people responsible for their deaths? How many innocent people had he caught because TESA labeled them terrorist?

His gut twisted at the thought. But he had to focus. Drake would soon arrive, and he had to figure out what to do. If this vid was a fake, it was an expert job. Too much detail and coincidences to be a fraud.

He realized his teeth had been grinding; he relaxed his jaw and faced Jaya. "If you lost everything, how did you buy your ship?"

Her eyes stared past him. "My birthday was a month before the murder. Mark, my husband, knew I wanted my own ship, and surprised me with it. We had barely registered it before the events on the vid. Rowl didn't know I had a ship docked at space port." She paused. "It's the only connection I have left to Mark and my family."

There was only one thing he could do if justice was to be served. "I'm taking you to Earth."

The laser cannon bore a hole into the fallen rock. Pieces fell away as the hole grew and outside light filled the cave. The dripping, liquid stone on the edges of the hole quickly hardened into a secure support for the passageway.

Men filed in, batons in hand. Gil stood to greet them. "Search the cave. She may have left evidence we'll need for the trial."

The leader nodded and motioned for the others to spread out.

Gil cut the cord wrapped around her legs and grabbed Jaya by the arm. "Time to meet justice, Miss Jinkins." They crawled through the hole and adjusted to the sunlight.

Sergeant Drake, along with another soldier, stood guard outside the cave's entrance.

Gil stopped and turned to him. "Thank you for the rescue, Sergeant. I'm sure it will be looked upon favorably by TESA. I'll put in a good word for you."

Drake's mouth curled upward as he approached Gil. "Inspector, I have orders from Commander Rowl to take possession of the prisoner." He thrust papers toward Gil.

Gil scanned them; they appeared valid, including Rowl's signature. He rebuked himself. He should have seen something like this coming.

Gil stared Drake in the eyes. "I'll only release the prisoner to Commander Rowl himself."

Drake's mouth broke into a full grin. "Sorry, Inspector. I have my orders, and you'll be in violation of yours if you don't turn her over."

Gil bore into Drake's eyes. He waited for a few seconds to pass. Drake's smile faded into a frown. Gil smiled and Drake's forehead wrinkled.

"Sergeant Drake, it is unfortunate that we couldn't come to a mutual agreement."

Drake's eyes widened.

He was there! The vid can't be a fake! Gil pulled his baton out and hit the shield button. The projected force knocked Drake off his feet, sending him flying through the air. He crashed onto the ground by the cave's entrance.

The other soldier whipped out his gun and a blast of energy electrified the air, then crackled against Gil's shield.

Drake had regained his feet, and shot his gas pistol in rapid fire. Flashes of sparks ricocheted off the shield as bullets burst into billows of green gas.

Gil projected the shield outward, shoving the gas away and slamming the two men against the rock face. While they were down,

Gil snatched his gas pistol and fired. One shot hit the soldier's forehead and gas erupted over him; he went limp. Another shot fired at Drake, but he rolled away before the bullet arrived.

Drake spun to his feet and pulled his baton, firing up his shield. He projected it outward to Gil's. The two shields crashed together, pushing Gil back as crackling energy filled the air. Drake lifted his shield and brought it down. Gil lurched forward as the pressure released, then jerked back as the shield smashed into his again. The force of the impact tore his baton from his hand, it rattled against the rocky cave entrance.

Drake smiled as he stepped toward them, the shield humming. He raised his wristband to his mouth. "This is Sergeant Drake, I need backup."

That's the last thing Gil needed. He slapped his hand on the ray gun, and blasted at the cave entrance. Rocks cracked and crashed in, sealing the hole. It'd take them twenty minutes at least to drill back out.

Drake's shield slammed into Gil. Searing heat mixed with pain crushed in upon him. His head swam for a moment, then he realized he lay on the ground several meters away. His whole body protested at the shooting pain. He scanned the area. Where had Jaya gone? Was she foolish enough to attempt an escape?

Drake approached. "I'm sorry it has to end this way, Inspector. Not my choice, you understand." He raised his shield baton to use it like a guillotine to cut Gil in half. Then he brought it down hard.

Gil forced himself to roll toward Drake; the shield's edge crackled into the dirt behind him. Gil leaped to his feet and threw himself at Drake. Drake swung his baton toward Gil's head; Gil raised his elbow and smashed Drake's fingers, causing him to drop the baton.

Drake's knee jammed into Gil's chest, sending him sprawling backwards as waves of pain washed over his ribs. Drake slid his ray gun out and pointed it at Gil. "You lose."

Jaya's arms flew up behind him, her bound wrist rolled over his head and she yanked him back by the neck. The ray blast fired to Gil's left.

Drake flung Jaya over his shoulder, wrapped an arm around her neck, and jammed the gun's barrel against her temple. "Now I can finish what I started. I don't think Rowl will care if she's alive or not."

Jaya's big eyes stared at Gil in pleas of help.

Gil stepped toward Drake. "Put the gun down."

"Get your hands away from your holster. Put 'em up in the air, or I'll fry her!"

Gil lifted his hands.

Drake smiled. "Well, what do you know. You like her."

"No. It's just I'm not a bloodthirsty, one-man lynch mob like you. She needs to have her day in court like anyone else." Gil caught an image of Drake's baton not far from his feet.

Jaya jerked against his hold. "I didn't do anything, you murderer!"

"Shut up!" Drake focused on her as he tightened his arm around her neck.

Gil glanced down at the baton. He kicked it around to point toward Drake, tapped the shield button with his boot's tip, then stepped on it.

The shield rammed into the pair, sending them sprawling to the ground. Gil dashed toward Drake before he had a chance to reorient himself, and slipped a couple of gas bullets from his belt. He fell toward Drake. Drake's eyes opened and his mouth gaped as Gil smashed the gas bullets onto Drake's forehead. The fragile tips burst and gas cloaked Drake's face.

Gil sucked in air to avoid the gas. Drake had too; Gil punched Drake in the stomach causing his air to spew forth. He sucked in, and his eyes glazed over and shut.

Gil leaped up and released his breath. He helped Jaya to her feet. "Sorry about that. I didn't have many options left."

She smiled and Gil saw appreciation instead of sarcasm for the first time. Jaya winked. "No problem...what's your name?"

"Gil." He dusted himself off. "You came back. Why?"

She shrugged. "It's not everyday I find someone willing to fight over me."

He chuckled. "It's not everyday I find someone who can fix the sickness of TESA." Gil sighed. "It won't be as easy to reach Earth now, however. They'll be watching for us. We'll have to sneak out of TESA space. Most likely they'll issue a warrant on us to the Terran authorities, with instructions to deport us back to TESA."

"Welcome to my life of late."

"You mean, welcome to life, period. You're like a light at the end of this dark tunnel of revenge."

One corner of her mouth curled upward. "Yes, life. Thank you."

Gil nodded, and led her toward *Susan*.

Fantasy Stories

Dragon Stew

"I plan to expand the *Angel Guard's Tactical Manual*," Earl stated matter-of-factly, "It hasn't been updated in eons."

"This is your first assignment, Earl. How on heaven can a newbie angel think to change the manual?" The corner of George's mouth turned up as he shook his head.

"Simple, my friend. I'm going to marry my assignment, Christopher the dragon-slayer, to your assignment, Argu the dragon."

George's mouth fell open; his eyes bulged. "Do you have any idea how silly that sounds? You're crazy if you think that'll work."

"George," Earl said, "These days a good guardian works outside the box to keep his assignment alive."

"Outside the box?" George shook his head. "You've been listening to nineteen-eighties, self-help seminars again, haven't you?"

"Hey, you should listen to them. Like, totally mind expanding stuff. Rad to the max, like, fer sure." Earl chuckled and seated himself in an easy chair constructed of clouds.

Earl swept his hand in front of him. "Just look at your office, George. White walls, white desk, white chairs, white staples and pens. The only color here is a photo on your desk of your Martian family vacation and the black coffee in your white cup. Face it, you're locked in a box."

George stared at his coffee cup and chuckled.

Earl continued, "I have a responsibility, to keep this dragon-slayer alive. He's in a dangerous business and needs intervention. I believe this will work. Then I'll stand out from the pack and Michael will beg to promote me!"

George moved toward Earl. "You'll stand out all right. Listen, these people's lives are not a stage you can play out your innovative scripts on. Study how the previous guardians protected him and do what they did. They succeeded."

"So if Christopher kills your assignment, Argu, I'll be successful?"

"Well, no, but you know what I mean. I've my assignment and you've yours. Argu's longevity isn't your concern."

"I see where you're going with this." Earl pointed a finger at George. "You desire him to be her dinner. Why am I talking to the competition?"

George sighed. "Earl, I'm not your opponent. You don't understand how this will affect other lives. The interwoven threads of heaven and earth are more complex than you think."

"All right then, how would you propose I handle this, huh?" Earl crossed his arms.

George paused. "Here's my best advice: Mercy's power towers above all else."

"See, instead of practical help, you spout platitudes."

"But it's true." George sat at his desk and sipped his *Jehoshaphat Java*. "Well, how do you propose to accomplish this marriage? I can't wait to hear this."

Earl didn't care for George's opinion, but his stare bore into him. "With the help of a wizard."

"A wizard? You know a wizard?"

"Yes and no. I don't know one, personally, but I can be one."

Earl stood. He raised his hands, cupped them, and formed a ball of light. He drew his hands apart and threw it over himself. Earl checked his clothing. It had changed into an old tattered cloak dotted by small stars, complete with a hood. He raised a hand to his face. He felt wrinkles and aged skin under his fingertips.

"Tada!" Earl said, "It's Dante, the greatest wizard of all ages!"

George shook his head. "You've got to be kidding. You'll do more damage than good. I say dump this idea before you create messes I'll have to deal with."

"Watch and learn my dear friend. Watch and learn what new ideas can accomplish!" Earl vanished before George could speak another word.

―――――――

Argu focused on the drip, drip of water in distant caverns. She yawned; a puff of fire escaped her nostrils. She stretched her red, scaly body and then curled her tail around her. Argu closed her eyes and drifted between sleep and wakefulness.

Sounds of footfalls rang in her sensitive ears. Argu's ears perked up. She watched the entrance through a nearly closed eye.

A hooded head peered into the cavern; its body followed. Argu could only see illuminated eyes from the face, but a beard flowed down to the creature's waist. Pale light from the entrance backlit the form and created a temporary radiance around the figure. It examined the treasure on the floor.

Argu tensed. She sprang to her feet and spread out her wings. "You're dumber than I thought, dragon-slayer. After I'm done with you, I'll enjoy your roasted flesh for dinner and pick my teeth with your leg bones." Argu displayed her razor sharp teeth in a grin. "Do you have any last words before I cook you for my evening meal?"

"Well, well. What a wonderful display, my Argu," the strange old man said.

"Your Argu? Who do you think you are?" Argu lowered her wings and raised her head.

The man pulled back his hood to reveal a scarred and wrinkled face. Unkempt, gray hair flowed over his shoulders.

"I'm a wizard. Can't you tell? And since I happen to be immortal, you can't kill me, so cool off. I'm here to help you after all. I'd appreciate more hospitality."

Argu stared at the old man. He displayed every stereotypical description of a wizard she had ever seen or heard. "Why would you decide to help me?"

The man scanned the room and sat on a rock formation protruding from the wall. "Because dragon-slaying breeds violence. It's so twelve-hundredish, time to dump this outdated practice."

Argu smiled. "Well, I'm for that." Her smile faded. "But how do I know this isn't a trap?"

"For starters, my name's Dante. I happened to pass through, advertising my wizardly services when I overheard talk at the tavern. They said a knight named Christopher plans to kill you."

"Yes, he's the one." Her face flushed at the mention of his name.

Dante pulled a pipe from his cloak and filled it with a heavenly-smelling tobacco. He patted his pockets then stared at Argu. "Do you have a light?"

Argu smiled showing her teeth.

"You know what I mean! You may not be able to kill me but you would still burn off my clothing. My naked cunning would be revealed." Dante smiled.

"Don't tempt me." She leaned her head close to Dante and pursed her lips. She puffed and a blue flame appeared from her mouth.

Dante placed his pipe under the fire and puffed until smoke floated over his head.

Argu waited while Dante puffed. She frowned. "Well, I assume you have a plan? Speak up wizard. Otherwise I'll go back to sleep."

"Yes I do, dear Argu. It'll involve a spell. You may not like it."

"If it will keep me from getting killed, I'm for it."

"Then let's refine our plan tonight. You, my Argu, will need to marry Christopher."

"What!" A flash of flames escaped her nostrils. "Are you out of your mind, wizard? Even if I could marry a human, the very thought of marrying him turns my stomach. And let me tell you, it takes a lot to turn a dragon's stomach."

"I knew you wouldn't like it," Dante said.

"Even if I decided to do it, how would you convince a dragon-slayer to marry me?"

"Argu, Argu. Are you not aware that wizards can brew love potions?"

Argu paused. "Well, yes, but tell me why I would desire him to fall in love with me?"

"It's quite simple. Once he's married you, he'll not be able to kill you. It's like an alliance. Then he'll leave you to live your life in peace for he cannot live with you."

"That's crazy. Exactly what are you smoking?"

Dante remained silent. He puffed on his pipe; the smoke rose to the cave ceiling.

Argu smiled. If he could do what he said, she could use this wizard's silly scheme to destroy the knight. "Lord, what a fool this immortal is."

"What?" Dante stiffened and glared at Argu.

"Oh, I said, 'what a foolishly clever plan of this immortal.'" She gave Dante a big grin. "But do you think this love potion of yours will make him love a big, old, scaly dragon like me?"

"No, but it should be sufficient if you're turned into a beautiful young woman, just his type." Dante smiled.

If he could do this, it would be perfect. She would have no problem getting close to the love-struck dragon-slayer. He would then become the slayee instead of the slayer. "You have a deal, wizard. When do we start?"

"Right now. I have the potion and spell with me. I overheard in the tavern he's planning to attack in a week. You'll have to seduce him into marriage before then."

"Then it's time to prove you are indeed a wizard by changing me into the woman of his dreams."

Dante drew one last puff from the embers of his pipe and put it away. He stood and removed a book from under his cloak.

"Hum, let's see." Crisp paper flipped through his fingers. Dante separated a couple stuck pages. "Here we are." Dante held out one hand toward Argu. "From the scales of a dragon to the pale color of a...," Dante raised the book closer to his eyes.

"What's wrong?"

"Oh, this is a new book." Dante glanced at Argu with an unsure smile. "I need to read the footnotes to ensure I change you into the right thing."

Argu rolled her eyes. He appeared old but acted as if he had learned magic yesterday.

"Ah, here it is, now hold still, this won't hurt a bit."

Hurt? Argu tensed.

"From the scales of a dragon to the pale color of ale in a flagon, make this beast enough for the love of man to feast!"

The wizard blurred for a second but sharpened back into focus. "That's horrible poetry. The meter's all off."

"It's not meant to be poetry. It's a spell you silly woman. The point is it works."

"It did?" She realized the wizard had grown to her size. No, she had shrunk to his size. Her voice sounded sweet instead of gruff. Her body had morphed into a woman's, like many she had seen. It seemed so thin, as if an ordinary beast could chomp right through it.

"I hope I don't have to fight in this body. It's not designed for it."

"No, but it is designed to attract Christopher's love." Dante stared at her. His lips formed a smile. "Yes, it's very well designed. I think we'd better obtain some clothing for you."

"Why?"

"You're attempting to attract one particular man, not every man in the village."

"Why would lack of clothing cause that?"

Dante threw up his hands. "Look, you'll need pockets to carry the potion."

"Oh, okay. Why didn't you just say so?"

Dante shook his head. "You remind me of Salome. Here, hold this love potion while I find a spell to create clothing for you."

"Salome?"

"Oh yea, an old ang—I mean, witch friend of mine. I guess you can use the name if you wish."

"Salome." She felt the way it rolled off her lips. "I like the sound of it. Salome it is." Argu smiled. It wouldn't be long before she'd have Christopher at her mercy.

Christopher ducked as the broad sword swooshed over his head. He thrust with his weapon to the chest, but missed. Christopher swung in a figure-eight pattern. Still, he struggled to gain the offensive. Frustrated, he fell for the feint to the right. He grimaced at the cutting pain on his belly.

"Owch! Mom, that hurt. Can't you be more careful?"

"Oh I'm sorry, dear. I lost myself in the moment." Her smile didn't communicate any regrets.

"If you slice my liver out, the dragon will be the least of my worries." He scanned his wound. She had drawn blood, a deep scratch.

"Neither will you fight the dragon well if your sixty-year-old mother can get the best of you."

"But I'm not sword fighting the dragon."

"How about your fiancée?" A sweet voice sang behind him.

Christopher turned to see Salome gliding over the grassy yard. Her reddish-brown hair shimmered in the sun like fire. His eyes followed her every move.

"Hello, Henrietta, how's your family?" Salome said.

"Oh fine, just fine. And yours?"

Salome opened her mouth, paused and then said, "Thank you, they're fine. They would like to meet you, but they're always too busy with their, ah, hearth business to travel much."

"Are you staying for dinner?" Christopher said.

"I would be glad to dine with you. I even brought more of the wine you like, dear." She lifted a bulging wineskin.

"Wonderful," Henrietta said, "I'll go get dinner ready. And don't you two be late either. Cold food makes for a cold heart."

Wineskin in hand, Henrietta left for the house.

As soon as Henrietta was out of sight, Christopher's arms locked with Salome's. Her skin felt smooth and soft, like velvet. Her long redish, brown hair whipped around his head in a gust of wind, embracing his heart and soul. Her lips pressed upon his and sent a tingling buzz through his limbs. It seemed like hours passed before they broke the spell for air.

"You're an answer to longing desire." The words flowed from the stirring of his heart.

But, instead of a loving response, loathing emanated from her expression.

Christopher wrinkled his brow. Did she love him or not? "Are my whispers nothing?"

He followed her eyes to the sword still in his hand. He placed it back in its sheath. "You've never liked this sword."

"I've no use for violence. I find it barbaric."

"I admit killing is ugly. We should avoid it if possible. Yet sometimes one has no choice, kill or be killed. That dragon's a killer."

"How do you know?" She stepped back, hands on hips.

"Because people often disappear for no reason. It must be the dragon. He has to eat."

"Maybe those disappearances aren't related to the dragon. Maybe she eats animals like you."

Christopher huffed. He couldn't believe she was taking the dragon's side. "Look, it's the way things are. Dragons burn and pillage. Someone has to stop them before people die."

"Have you or anyone else seen this dragon burn and pillage?"

Christopher scratched his head. "Well, no, but it doesn't matter. We all know he will."

Salome rolled her eyes. "I don't know that. You don't even know the gender of the dragon. You might be killing an innocent animal, a very misunderstood animal."

She seemed to have plenty of maybes and mights. "I have no choice. I have a reputation to uphold."

Her eyes narrowed. "That reputation is nothing and you'll get nothing from it."

Christopher clenched his teeth and turned his back to her. She had questioned his chosen profession. Yet, he lacked valid counterarguments to answer her common-sense points. Then he heard a sigh and felt her hand on his back.

"I'm sorry. I didn't mean to frustrate you." She rubbed his neck. "Let's join your mother. Perhaps I can help her with dinner."

He felt the tension drain from him. She had a magical way of helping him over his emotional frustrations, even those she created.

A week had passed since they'd met, yet they acted like a couple who had been together for years. He couldn't wait to marry her.

"You go ahead." He squeezed her hands. "I'll be there in a moment. First I need to pray and think."

"Very well, my love, I'll see you after a while." She glided toward the house. Christopher watched trance-like until she disappeared from view.

Christopher turned and strolled alongside the forest's edge, head down. "God, what am I to do about this dragon if not prevent him from killing innocent people? Or, could Salome be right? Did the dragon kill people? Is my job pointless and cruel? Is the real choice before me whether to be a dragon-slayer or not?"

He spent several minutes in prayer before he retired to the house for dinner.

Salome and Henrietta talked long into the night. As Salome had hoped, Henrietta invited her to stay the night rather than take the dark road home. She huddled under blankets in a spare bed. Less than an hour passed before Henrietta and Christopher snored away on the other side of the room.

Salome arose and tip toed across the floor to Christopher's bed. Her plan had succeeded so far. Now she would finish it.

She stared at the snoring knight before her. She had not expected him to be so charming and loveable. She longed to marry him and live happily ever after.

Yet, even if they did marry, once he found out the truth, there could be no happily ever after. She sighed at the lost possibility.

His sword hung on a peg by his bed. She unsheathed it and held it in her hands. It shimmered in the moonlight. A feeling of authority and respect, confidence and safety coursed through her heart. What a wonderful sword!

Then in her mind, she heard the distant dragon voices this weapon had killed. Joy and power morphed into revulsion and fear. She held the broad sword over his bed. The voices grew louder: "Blood for blood, give us justice."

The weapon rose into the air; it quivered in the moonlight. If she killed him, wouldn't she bear his guilt? Maybe, but at least no more dragons would die at his hands. She could not allow her desire for him to prevent the execution of justice. She pulled the sword up farther and tensed her muscles.

She plunged the weapon to its target. Before it could draw blood, a bright light burst forth between her and him. She lost her footing, fell backwards, and collapsed with a thud without losing her grip on the sword. The light formed into what Salome could only call an angel.

"My dear," said the bright man, "Sorry I scared you, but I couldn't let you kill him."

"Who are you?" Her heart pounded in her chest.

"I'm your guardian angel. The name's George."

"You mean, dragons have guardian angels?" She stood.

"Of course, all living creatures do."

Her voice quivered. "How come so many die then? How come you don't stop people like him from killing dragons?" She stared at the knight. His peaceful sleep contrasted with her chaotic emotions.

"He'll die in due time, but you shouldn't ruin your life."

"What if I decide it's his time to die anyway?" Her grip on the sword tightened.

"You see, that's why so many dragons die. I can divert you temporarily or try to convince you not to kill him, but I can't stop you anymore than I can stop all the other dragon-slayers from killing their prey." George moved closer to her. "A dead dragon-slayer will not solve anything."

She relaxed her grip on the sword, the tip lowered. "You're right." She faced the angel. "If I killed him, it would only provoke others to arise and take his place in greater numbers. I let my emotions get the better of me." She shuddered at what she had almost done. Her heart welled up for Christopher. "I'll not kill him, he's my only love born from my only hate."

George peered into her eyes. "You should be all right now." George vanished and the room darkened until her eyes adjusted to the dim moonlight.

She examined the sword in her hand and then Christopher. He wouldn't be able to slay dragons without his sword. Even if he bought a new one, he wouldn't be comfortable going to the dragon's cave with an untried weapon. Superstitions about such things abounded with knights.

With sword in hand, she slipped into the cool night air. Cricket-chirps filled the forest along with an occasional hoot from an owl. The moonlight lit the trail back to her cave.

———————

A warm sun hung on the horizon. The crisp morning smelled of daffodils. The trees bordering the yard rustled in the gentle breeze. He would win a unique victory today; he felt it in his bones.

He swung his sword in patterns his teachers had taught him. Sleepiness disappeared and blood flowed in his veins. The time to face the dragon in battle drew near.

He halted his practice when Salome appeared over the hill. She had a bounce in her step and a smile on her lips. But by the time she reached him, she wore a frown and wrinkled brow.

"Ah, my dear Salome, there you are."

"Hi." She stared at the sword in his hand. "Your sword seems different than the one you had yesterday, isn't it?"

"I did clean it last night for the coming fight." He turned it over in his hand. "However, I keep a practice sword by my bed for protection. When I awoke this morning, I found an empty sheath. I don't recall having used it lately. Did you see it when you left this morning?"

"Practice sword?" Her eyes widened.

"Yes, this one I've taken into every dragon battle and it has never failed me. Without it, I wouldn't dare attack the dragon." Christopher jabbed the weapon into the air. "With my faithful sword that dragon doesn't stand a chance. Heat up the kettle, 'cause tonight we'll feast on dragon stew!"

Her face burned red. "Sure, a new sword will stop you, but not the killing of innocent life."

Christopher groaned. "Do we have to rehash that again?"

"Oh no, let's not bother with stupid things like reason and kindness. Just kill, kill, kill!" She turned and stomped up the hill.

"Where are you going?" Christopher wondered at the sudden changes. She reacted like an unpredictable beast. Your best friend one moment and biting your head off the next.

"I just remembered something I need to do. I'll see you later," she said without turning around.

He figured a little levity might calm her down.

"Until we meet again. Separation is such a bright sadness!" He swung one arm into the air and placed the other on his chest. She still didn't turn around.

Christopher shrugged his shoulders. He'd have to deal with her later. The coming fight with the dragon demanded his attention. He swung his sword in an arc but lost his grip. It sailed through the air and embedded in an oak.

"Hum, at least I've struck fear into the trees."

Christopher peered into the clearing. The cave opening burrowed into a two-hundred-foot barren hill. Tuffs of grass dotted the otherwise dirt and rock floor. The afternoon sun heated Christopher's armor. The smell of pungent sweat filled the cramped suit.

"Argu, O Argu, where are you Argu?" Christopher whispered as he tiptoed toward the entrance to the cave. He listened for the crack of twigs and the crunch of dry leaves as he scanned the area.

"Christopher." A voice from behind startled him.

Christopher slipped as he turned and crashed to the ground in a heap. He saw Salome over him. "So much for surprising the dragon." He banged his fist on the ground. "What are you doing here, Salome?"

"I'm waiting to find out myself." She seemed to hold back a laugh.

He reached out for her hand and she helped him back to his feet as his armor clanked and rattled. Christopher wondered why the dragon hadn't stirred from his lair.

"You should go back to the village. You could get hurt here," he said.

"Tell me about it. You're the one intending to do the hurting."

"When are you going to drop that arguement?" He felt like a weight had fallen on him. "You're distracting me. Go back to the house and wait for me."

"I'm waiting for someone."

"Who? The dragon? Are you friends with the dragon? Is that why you're against me killing him?"

"You could say—"

"Salome, I see everything's going according to my plan." Dante appeared from behind a tree.

"You know this man?"

"Only for a few days." She faced Dante. "Whether your plan will work remains to be seen, wizard."

"He's here now. We can conduct the marriage."

"Marriage!" Christopher jerked his head toward the wizard.

"Yes, you heard right." Dante nodded.

"Are you crazy? The dragon could dash out and eat us alive while we kiss. Besides, you're not a minister, you're a wizard."

"Though this appears crazy, I have a logical plan. Now let's begin." Dante pulled a book from under his cloak and flipped through pages.

He rubbed the crease open and read, "Gather together an eye of newt, toe of frog, wool of bat, tongue of dog—oh, I'm sorry. This spell turns handsome princes into toads. Oh dear, that was close." He flipped through more pages.

"But that's not a spell," Salome said.

Dante ignored her.

"Look, Mr. Wizard, I don't think this is a good time for a wedding." Christopher glanced at the cave.

"Don't worry about the dragon. I guarantee you she'll not be appearing." Dante's head popped up. He smiled. "At least not till we're done."

Christopher opened his mouth but paused. "Well, if you say so." Christopher faced Salome. "I planned on marrying you after finishing this job. Since the dragon's not here, I suppose we can tie the knot now."

Salome didn't say anything but shook her head affirmatively. He thought she seemed nervous, but who wouldn't be before a marriage.

"Very well," Dante said, "let's get this underway. Dearly beloved, we are gathered here today in the sight of God—" He glanced at the sky. "And man, to join together this man and this dra—I mean, woman in holy matrimony. Do you promise to hold each other in sickness and in health, yada, yada, yada? Of course you do. I now pronounce you man and wife. You may kiss the bride."

Christopher wrapped Salome in his arms and kissed her with joy. Then she changed. His arms could no longer hold her. Her skin sprouted rough scales. Instead of soft lips, he felt hard teeth. Christopher stumbled back.

In place of the beautiful woman, a dragon stood before him, the very one he planned to kill. "What devilry is this? Where is Salome? Did you eat her?"

"Christopher, my love." Argu's gruff voice vibrated him. "I am your wife. I am, or was, Salome."

"No, this cannot be." He stepped back to steady himself against a tree.

"It is her, I assure you Christopher," Dante said, "I cast a spell on the dragon, turning her into a woman and gave her a love potion to seduce you. She has succeeded very well. Now she's your wife, therefore you cannot kill her." Dante stuffed the book into his cloak and prepared to leave.

Christopher fixed his eyes on the dragon, then on the wizard, and back again on the dragon. "No, I cannot accept this."

"Love should look with the mind, not the eyes," Argu said with a grin, "I'm sure we can obtain a very big bed for the cave."

Christopher narrowed his eyes and gritted his teeth. "I'll have none of it. If a wizard can conduct a marriage, then a knight can execute a divorce." Christopher unsheathed his sword and charged.

Argu leapt and a gust of wind pushed against Christopher with the beat of her wings. He launched into the air. His sword tip only touched her scales as she rose. He crashed upon a rock formation, armor banging together.

"I told you this wouldn't work!" she said to Dante.

Dante pulled his hood tight over his head. "Oh my, oh dear, what went wrong with my plan? Ricky and Lucy never had fights like this. I don't understand."

Argu circled high into the sky and dove to the forest opening. "If you'll not leave me alone, even as your wife, I've no choice but to kill you, dragon-slayer." Argu flew low over the clearing and exhaled a trail of fire-breath.

Christopher flung himself out of the fire's path and into the cave entrance. He watched Argu climb for another pass. Christopher sheathed his sword and climbed the hill.

"Crazy fool," Argu said, "you cannot easily dodge my fire while climbing the side of a hill in a suit of armor."

She swooped to the ground; dust billowed under her. She raced up the side of the hill toward Christopher and exhaled a stream of fire.

Christopher jumped backwards from the hill. The rear and legs of his armor grew hot as Argu flew under him. He grabbed her neck and landed on her back with a loud grunt.

"Wow," Dante said, "Impressive!"

Christopher squeezed tight around Argu's neck. Wind rushed through his helmet. She flew high, dove to the ground, careened through turns and spun upside down. He barely kept his grip; his arms ached.

Two minutes seemed forever. But Christopher sensed the dragon weakening. He pried his right arm from around the dragon, drew his sword and placed it under her neck.

"Off with your head!" His muscles tightened and he pulled up, but his sword only found air. He discovered his legs now straddled Salome's back; she had changed back to a woman.

Without the advantage of wings, they both plummeted to the soil. Grunts and screams poured forth as they slammed into the ground. Flying sections of armor rattled and a wall of dust arose. They rolled for several yards until they crashed into the trunk of an oak tree.

Christopher arose and gritted his teeth against the pain. He picked up his sword from the ground and limped toward Salome. The love potion had worn off.

"You wouldn't kill your own wife would you?" She begged with her eyes.

He refused to melt. "You may be my wife, but you're not a woman. I cannot be married to a dragon." He prepared to drive the sword through her heart.

"Dante, do something! Why did you change me back?"

"It wasn't me. There must be something wrong with this spell. Oh dear."

"No." A voice echoed from the other side of the clearing. "Dante didn't change her, I did." An angelic light grew in the clearing until a man in white robes stood before them.

"Who are you? An angel of some kind?" Christopher said.

"My name's George. I'm this dragon's guardian angel."

"This dragon has a guardian angel? No wonder I'm unable to slay him." Christopher glanced at Salome. "I mean, her."

"There's your guardian, Christopher." George pointed to Dante.

"A wizard is my guardian angel?" Christopher wrinkled his brow. "What happened? Does God now barter the job of guardian angel to mercenaries?"

George waved his hand toward Dante. The black cloak turned to white robes, the hood melted into silver hair and light dissolved the dark appearance.

"Eh, hi Christopher," Earl said.

"You're working for him!" Salome's eyes burned toward Earl. "If I had my dragon-breath now—"

"What kind of guardian angel are you?" Christopher said, "You married me to a dragon. What were you thinking?"

"I thought you would both live happily ever after. Love stories always end happily." Earl displayed a sheepish smile.

"You've been watching too much television," George said.

"Television?" Christopher stared at George. "Whatever your television said, it doesn't change what I must do." Christopher turned back to face Salome. She cowered in fear against the tree as Christopher raised the sword.

"Hold on, Christopher," George said, "She can never go back to being a dragon. I permanently changed her to this form."

Christopher remained fixed on his prey. His sword hovered in the air. He moved his hand toward her, but an invisible force pushed back. He tried again but could not bring the sword's tip more than a quarter inch from her heart.

"Stop preventing me from killing her!" Christopher said.

"We're doing nothing to stop you," George said, "You can't kill her because you love her."

Such a thought hadn't crossed his mind. Christopher dug into his heart. He tore through the hate of dragons, through the fear of death, through the prestige of his position as dragon-slayer, down into the core of his being and the beat of his heart. There he found true love aflame for Salome.

Christopher felt his determination softened to compassion and then to love. A love concocted not by spell or potion, but a love born from a person he cared about rather than a beast to kill. He lowered the sword and slumped against the tree next to her.

Relief beamed on Salome's face. She hugged the battered knight and he responded by drawing her into his arms and kissing her forehead.

Salome settled her eyes on Christopher. "When I agreed to this deception, I hated you. Yet, you won my heart for who you are. If you'll have me, I could think of nothing I desire more than to live my life with you."

"The angel spoke the truth. I do love you." He held her tighter. "Even though this means my dragon-slaying days are over, I have no choice. I can do nothing else but be your husband."

She responded by hugging back. Joy radiated from her face. "Real love flows over sharp rocks before it meanders into pleasant lakes. So our love has flowed."

Christopher smiled. Then his eyes widened. "My grandfather forges metal. He could teach me to forge swords."

"So people can go out and kill more dragons?"

"People use swords to kill people more than they do dragons."

"Oh. Then I'm okay with it."

Christopher hugged Salome. "Come, let's return to my house. I'll tell Mom, 'Look, I went to slay a dragon and I came back married to one.'" They both laughed as they arose. Salome supported the knight as he limped home.

Earl watched as Christopher and Salome hobble out of sight.

"Now see, George, it all worked out just like I planned. They're happy and both still alive."

"What a piece of work this angel is." George gazed at the sky and shook his head.

"What?"

"You really think they're going to live happily ever after?"

"Sure, all's well that ends well."

George turned to face Earl, a smirk on his face. "Just wait till you see their children."

Once you have tired of trying to find all twenty-one Shakespearian quotes, you can use the Shakespeare-Dragon Stew Key at http://www.copple.us/DS-ShakespeareKey.html to see how many you found and which you missed.

Facing the Cave

"And though countless have tried," the bard said to the tavern audience, "The dragon that never dies continues to devour all who come to its cave."

Galak clapped with the people but noticed Sir Humblart, his teacher and friend, stared as if into another world. When Galak saw Sir Humblart's jaw set, he knew the story had stirred a desire in his master. Galak took another gulp from his stein in hopes of numbing the rising fear.

Sir Humblart rose from his seat. "Come, Squire. We have a dragon to slay."

The bard laughed. "Didn't you hear me? This dragon is death itself. No man can defeat death."

Sir Humblart smiled and his eyes lit as they always did when he would say something of importance. "Correct, no man can if no one attempts it."

"Attempt away! The dragon is always hungry." Laughter erupted from the patrons.

Sir Humblart nodded. "And if I return from death, then what?"

The bard stumbled over words then blurted out, "I'll believe that when I see it!" More guffaws arose.

Sir Humblart downed the last of his ale and motioned for Galak to follow.

After grabbing supplies, Sir Humblart led Galak through the forest toward the undefeated foe.

"Sir, I have your sword," Galak said.

Sir Humblart didn't turn his head. "I'll have no cause for such weapons. Keep hold of it. You will need it."

Their feet crunched the dirt and dried leaves on the forest floor as they pushed toward—what? His death? Galak watched the armor-clad knight marching resolutely to face the monster that had sent so many to hell's gates. No hint of fear twitched across his face. No evidence of second thoughts surfaced in those coal-black, unblinking eyes.

In due time, they entered the clearing where the dragon's cave bore into the mountain. Strewn across the knoll lay scorched armor and rusted swords. Bones rested thick across the grass, piled by the cave opening. Many lives had been spent attempting to destroy the dragon.

A roar erupted from beneath the earth, and the ground shook. Smoke belched from the entrance as if dust long undisturbed exploded from its cloisters. Mournful cries underlay the horrific noise; Galak wanted to cry with them.

Galak fled behind a tree as he watched the beast burst from the cave and land a few feet from Sir Humblart. A mélange of greens and browns shimmered in the sunlight on its hide. The slender body tapered to a tail, which whipped to and fro. The other end held aloft a neck three times as long as any man's body. At the end of the neck, a broad head examined Sir Humblart with fiery eyes, and a forked tongue lashed the air.

"Sir, flee before it's too late," Galak yelled out.

Sir Humblart turned to Galak. "To free them, I must die." He faced the dragon, his feet together, lifted his arms as if to fly, and cast his head forward.

Now Galak knew his master had lost his mind. Perhaps the villagers brewed a stouter ale than they had realized. He cowered behind the tree as a deafening roar caused him to cover his ears in pain. But he couldn't remove his gaze from Sir Humblart.

The beast's head dove, and its open mouth scooped in Sir Humblart. Its head flung back. Galak watched as a bulge slid down the dragon's neck. Apparently satisfied with its meal, the dragon lumbered to the cave.

Galak's stomach twisted, and bile rose up his throat. Hot tears rolled down his cheeks. Then he remembered: he still had the sword. He could yet save his master and friend. An attempt likely ending in death, but love demanded no less. He steeled himself, unsheathed the weapon, drew himself to his feet, and prepared to charge.

The dragon halted before reaching the cave. A mournful cry shattered the air, and the dragon thrashed about, as if attempting to throw an invisible rider. It spun and writhed until another shriek filled Galak's ears. He fell to his knees; the sword dropped to the ground.

The dragon teetered and fell over onto its side with a ground-shaking crash. Galak peered at it, but the dragon no longer moved.

The ground rumbled until a blast of air exploded from the cave and twirled into a vortex. Galak swore he heard joyous singing within the gale. The bones around him rattled before the swirling wind sucked them into its grip, and they flew beyond the mountain and into the sky.

The pull of the music and push of the wind encouraged Galak. He crept toward the beast, eying it through wind-whipped hair, ready to flee, but it did not move. Not until Galak came close enough, did he see a bulge pushing against the skin.

He gasped and stumbled in haste to retrieve the sword. He raced back to the carcass and swung the sword two-handed upon the base of the neck. Green blood spewed forth, and with it the dragon's body vomited out Sir Humblart, covered in chunky, pea-green slime.

In his acid-seared hand, Sir Humblart held a heart the size of a grown man's head. He arose and cast a bright gaze upon Galak.

"No man can escape death. It can only be defeated from within. And now, I have destroyed it." Sir Humblart cast the heart into the cave.

Galak's pulse quickened as Sir Humblart's eyes pierced through him. The master turned and proceeded down the path to the village.

Galak followed, as he had always done—but now, through death to life.

Voices

Kyle relished the cool morning wind whipping through his hair. The purr of the convertible's motor blending with the whine of the transmission reminded Kyle he didn't own this car.

Visitors to the mental hospital would sometimes leave their cars unlocked. He jumped at such opportunities to get away. To speed to the only place he could find where the voices couldn't haunt him.

Is this as fast as you can go? Zach's voice sounded like fingernails on a chalkboard.

He's already racing, don't encourage him, Wanda said.

Kyle pushed down on the pedal. The tires squealed around a curve.

See? Wanda said. *You're going to get us killed.*

"He's not the only one who pushed me!" Kyle banged his fist on the dash. "Shut up! Both of you."

Kyle, you know we can't stop, Zach said.

Some appreciation for attempting to save your hide, Wanda said.

Kyle banged his fist on his forehead. "Go away, leave me alone!"

Seconds ticked by.

Can you make us go away? I don't think so! Zach's laugh rang in his head.

Kyle narrowed his eyes and gritted his teeth. He only had to survive for a few more minutes. Just stay sane, that's all he had to do.

Wanda giggled. *He's right, Kyle. You carry us with you everywhere. You cannot silence us.*

"That's what you think," Kyle said. Just around the curve, redemption would meet him: home.

You're delusional, Kyle. Delusional, I tell you. Zach's words echoed in his mind. *Don't fight us. Listen to—*

Kyle rounded a corner. His childhood home burst into view. Images from the past flooded his mind. The man crashing through the door, knife in hand. Dad attempting to defend them. The man overpowering him. Mom's screams ringing in Kyle's ears. The knife flashing in the lamplight. Her last word: "Run!"

Tears rolled down his cheeks as his eyes focused on the abandoned house that now lay in ruins. Peeling paint, broken windows, sagging roof, and a buckled wall stood among weeds that appeared to have digested sections of the house.

It had been twenty years since the day his life had turned into a nightmare. They put him into protective custody. The voices haunted him, woke him, taunted him. The custodial parents eventually admitted him to the mental hospital. But at this house, time appeared to roll back and the voices would disappear.

He pulled into the circle drive. Kyle plowed through the waist-high weeds to the back of the house. The tombstones of his parents protruded from the ground at an angle, jerking tears to his eyes. Waves of fear, regret and anger mixed to form an emotional tornado churning in his soul.

"I see you have returned, sonny. Would you like some cookies and milk?"

Kyle jerked his head up and smiled, "Granny, it's so good to see you." Granny lived next door and provided Kyle with many fond memories. Retired, she would join him in his adventures by the creek as a kid. Now, her arms, bones with skin draped over them, wobbled on her cane as she took deliberate steps.

Kyle followed Granny to her house and sat down for cookies and conversation. He always enjoyed his chats with her. Unlike the voices, she bathed him in pleasant conversation as she had always done.

"Granny—" She had paused for a moment. "You know those voices I hear in my head? Why do they stop when I'm here?"

She stared at the ground until Kyle feared she had fallen asleep. Her head bobbed up, as if she had to get a running start. "I ain't no shrink, but I think them voices you're a-hearin' are tryin' to keep you from a-seein' something about yourself. When you're here, you see it, so they no longer talk."

"I just want to live in my house." Kyle stuffed a cookie in his mouth, lamenting not all solutions tasted as good.

Granny lifted her bony hand and touched Kyle on his chest. "Sonny, if you'd deal with the memories inside, you could be freed from them voices."

They sat in silence, slurping milk and crunching cookies. "I wish you worked at the hospital. You're smarter than my shrink."

A knock at the door interrupted them. Kyle's heart sank. Granny arose and hobbled to the door. Two men in white coats and pants stood at the threshold.

"Mr. Kyle Winsome, you need your medications." They moved into the room, plastic restraining straps at the ready.

"No, I want to stay here! Don't make me go back. Don't make me leave here. The voices, they'll come back. Please!"

The men ignored his pleas. They jumped on him as he backed to the kitchen door. Kyle struggled, but could not escape. They bound him and dragged him out the door.

Kyle stared wide-eyed at Granny. "Granny, save me?" He knew she could do nothing. But he asked anyway.

She stood, one hand over her mouth. "Sonny, I'll be here next time you visit." She waved weakly.

Kyle watched helplessly from the back window, past the convertible that followed the van. His house disappeared behind the trees.

Kyle, we're back. Did you miss us? Did you think you would get rid of us this time?

Kyle could picture the smirk on Zach's face.

Kyle, Wanda said, *We want to help you, why did you disappear? I don't like it when you leave us.*

"No! Go away!" Kyle's hands turned white as he gripped the window's edge. Tears stained his cheeks. "No more voices!"

Sorry, Kyle, they both said together, *You can't stop us. We are you.*

Kyle froze. His eyes widened in realization of the truth. Granny was right. A smile creased his lips and he loosened his grip on the window sill.

"Yes, you are me. And that means I *can* silence you."

Wheel of Curses

I mumbled a spell as the aged woman spun the wheel. Most avoided the wheel at the carnival, but I could use magic to make the wheel stop where I wanted. I had learned much from an old wizard before he retired.

I had my eye on a prize: a magic wand. Other slots on the old wooden wheel contained curses, like becoming a goat or pig, some as horrible as a wart on someone's face.

But I ignored those. I had control. I could make the wheel stop where I wanted.

The wheel slowed to reveal its chipped paint. Some pictures I could barely make out. But the clicking of the wooden poles against the flap became more distinct, and the wand moved ever closer. It slowed to a crawl. The flap bent upon the pole separating the wand from my hand and paused on the tip. Then it slipped back to the previous slot.

I gasped. Someone had another spell on it. I gazed at the picture covered in peeling paint. Though weathered, I could make out an image of a fly.

I watched the lady. Her gray hair and pointy hat gave her the stereotypical appearance of a witch. Now I wondered if it was more than a costume at a carnival.

"I'm not really going to become a fly, am I?"

"Josh, wasn't it?"

I nodded.

She shook her head. "No, these are prizes." She reached back and pulled out a jar with a fly in it. "Here, come try again!"

I put the jar up to the sun and saw a fly buzzing around. "Great, I get a fly." I briefly thought about trying again, but if I couldn't control the wheel it would be too risky. Better to count myself lucky and leave while I could.

I strolled onto the fairway, thinking about the fly. Might as well release it; it's no use to me. So I uncovered the top and let the fly buzz out.

It landed on my arm. I stared at it and it looked back at me.

"I wonder what it's like to be a fly?"

Do you really want to know?

I blinked and shook my head. "Did you say that, fly?"

Yes. Thank you for freeing me. We have such short lives as it is.

"You're welcome."

Now, let's switch.

"Switch?"

The world blurred into a swirl of colors. My view changed into a fuzzier image, but clearly a head filled my sight. I swiveled my eyes around and received a clearer picture. My face stared at me.

Smells and wind pressure flowed down antenna and from my feet, six of them. I could see movement all around, though only certain areas focused clearly. And the colors appeared weird. Reds had disappeared, leaving blue and green tainted pictures whirling across my view.

"Wow, you can see pretty well with these eyes," the fly using my face said.

You mean, my eyes.

"Yes, your eyes." A smile grew on his face. "Then again, maybe they should be my eyes."

I felt the air pressure around me grow, and I instinctively beat my wings and flew away, escaping just as the hand slapped the arm.

I zipped through the air. The fly in my body chased after me. I found a spot to land. All the sensations, odd images, I couldn't make sense of them all. Then I saw my body approach. Two fingers protruded in front of me. I tried to move, but the fly body didn't respond. The fingers drew near, then one shot out to hit me. My world went black.

I awoke on the ground, still in a fly body. I saw my body looking for me, scanning the dirt and grass. I tried to recall any spell that might free me. No fly spells arose in my erratic thoughts.

Then his eyes caught sight of me as I lay in a swath of grass. I couldn't move. I lay in a shadow, and the cold air sapped all the strength I had. I could barely crawl.

I felt air pressure coming from two different places, but could do nothing to save myself. I would have opened my compound eyes wider if I could have. Just reverse the spell!

One spell too far, one spell too many, one spell undone, one spell no longer.

I heard my hands slamming together. I pulled them up to see the guts of a fly staining my palm. I breathed a sigh and rubbed the evidence of murder onto the grass.

I wondered if magic really gave me more control, or simply controlled me? I wouldn't make that assumption again.

Confessions of a Zombie's Wife

The funeral was a gas. No, I meant that literally. No sooner had we gathered around the site, than we smelled gas. The diggers had hit a gas line the company forgot to mark. Before we knew it, the area had been taped off by the police and crews of gas company workers repaired the breach. As I watched in a high-rise, with binoculars, they lowered Jim's casket into the ground and shoved the dirt over it with their machines.

"Sorry for your loss," Dominique said with his characteristic Jamaican accent. He worked with me at the office.

I didn't respond. The bulldozer knocking over Jim's grave stone held me in its stony grip.

"Darlene, are you going to be all right?" He placed a hand on my shoulder.

I let the binoculars hang from my neck. "The only way I can answer that is to kill your spouse and then you'll get the idea."

No, I didn't really say that. I wanted to, but instead I said, "Yeah, I'll be fine. I just need a good book to read. Then I'll be fine. Just fine."

That seemed to make him feel better, at any rate. The "funeral" being over, we left the observation roof of the high rise. I roamed the grocery store aimlessly, getting mostly junk food, and some horridly bitter coffee from a popular coffee house. Now I know why people like it so much. It goes with depression. Who wants good tasting coffee when everything is going downhill?

I stopped by Mom's to pick up our two children: Jake and Jill. One and three respectively. Mom said they should go to the funeral.

"Mom, they're not going to remember anything. They're too young."

"But it's their daddy. They should be there."

"And what am I suppose to do when Jake wants to breast feed? 'Excuse me Pastor, don't pay me any attention. Just business I need to take care of?'"

She grunted and frowned.

"Besides, you'll have to miss the funeral if they don't go."

That seemed to make her happy, and she didn't mention it again.

The rest of the evening mostly dealt with getting home, cooking dinner for the kids—most of it ending up on the floor, much to the delight of Fifi, our Doberman, and—oh, why Fifi? Silly really. Jim wanted a big manly dog. I wanted a poodle. We compromised. He picked the dog; I picked the name. Revenge can be sweet, sometimes.

At long last, I sat down in my favorite easy chair, with a cup of stale, burnt coffee to sooth my woes, and a book to lose myself in—off the NY Times best seller list: *Alien Dragons of the Dead from Outer Space*. A real thriller as it turned out.

Looking back, I probably should have realized the foreshadowing in that selection. From that moment, the remainder of my waking hours evolved into its own thriller. No sooner had I cracked open the book and read the first line, "It was a dusky and drizzly night," when I heard a knock at the door.

Well, not really a true knock. More like someone ran into the door. Lightening flashed through the windows, thunder clapped overhead, and the thud on the door came again.

I put my book down and peered out the peek hole. Couldn't see much as our porch light had burnt out. Then lightening flashed, and I gasped. I flung the door open, and there he stood.

Jim still dressed in the suit we had buried him in earlier that day, hair in a mess, dirt caked everywhere, and his eyes—as if they saw but didn't. They looked at me, but seemed to look past me as well. No sign of recognition crossed his face. But he retained a blank look as if trapped in a non-responsive body. Must have been the gas leak.

"Would you like some coffee? Happen to have some made." I stood to the side to allow him to come in.

"Uhhhh," was all he said.

"Okay, I'll take that as a yes." I headed to the kitchen to get a cup and he followed. Sort of. More like, he could barely bend his knees, so he moved like a running back whose muscles had grown so big he could only wobble down the field.

I had barely made it to the door of the kitchen when Fifi bounded out to meet Jim. He leaped up to lick his face. Well, that's what I thought at the moment. Instead Fifi took a bite out of Jim's arm. For some reason, Jim didn't seem to mind. At least it made a good chew toy for Fifi.

I poured him a cup of java and set down at the table with my own. He lumbered into a seat, and splashed the coffee over his face, getting some in his mouth. He always was a messy eater. Often worse than the kids. Then it dawned on me. Not sure why it took so long, but perhaps it was the lack of blood flowing from the bite Fifi took out of him.

"You're not really alive, are you?"

"Uhhhhug."

I shrugged.

"Uhhh, uhhhh, uhg." He waved one arm in the air.

"Oh, I see. You are, but you aren't. You're a zombie."

He nodded his head.

"Oh, silly me. You must be hungry after spending all day in that little box. Would you like something to eat?"

His eyes actually took on some desire at that point. He cocked his head to one side and seemed to really focus on me. I figured that was a good sign. It wasn't.

"I know that look, Jimmy boy. I miss you too!" I hopped out of my chair, ran around the table, and wrapped my arms around his smelly, rotting body.

He grabbed my hand and squeezed. Then took a bite.

"Ouch!" I pulled my hand away and saw the blood drooling down my arm. I slapped him with my other hand and he seemed taken aback, even as he licked the blood off his lips.

"Don't you know, you should never bite the hand that feeds you." I pulled out the first-aid kit and bandaged the wound as I contemplated my situation. "You know, Jim, we could make this work. I mean, I need a husband and you need a food source, right?"

He nodded with a grunt.

"I know you're the walking dead now, but I figure that's better than a non-walking dead husband, eh? So, I'll have the butcher order a lot of cows brains. Zombies like brains, right?"

"Uuuh," he shook his head.

"You don't like brains?"

"Uuhu."

"Oh, you don't care for cow brains. Then what kind?"

"Uhhhhh." He pointed at my head.

"My brains?"

He shook his head and jabbed his finger my direction a couple times. "Uhhhuhhh, uh!"

"Oh, you mean human brains."

He nodded vigorously.

"Well, that might be hard to pull off." I sat in the chair and took another sip of bitter brew for comfort and hopefully brain power.

"We do have a chain saw in the garage. I suppose I could lure people into our house, and you could attack them and use them for food."

He nodded as he stared off into space. "Uhmmmm."

"Then again, I recall a movie with that plot and it didn't work out for them in the end. Besides, I would run out of friends pretty quick."

He cocked his head to one side. Behind his eyes, it almost seemed he was laughing. I ignored it.

"Look, Jim, what we need—"

The doorbell rang.

"Who could that be at this hour?" I arose and answered the door.

"Dominique, what a pleasant surprise." I motioned for him to come on in.

"Darlene, I wanted to check on you, make sure everything is okay."

"Oh, everything is wonderful. Jim's back."

He blinked and then sighed. "Darlene, don't worry, many people have trouble letting go. It's—"

"No, I mean he's really back. Come and see." I lead him to the kitchen.

He peaked in and saw Jim sitting on the chair.

"Jim, wave hi to Dominique."

Jim stuck an arm straight into the air and waved.

Dominique stepped back. "Darlene, how can that be? He doesn't look right."

"Oh, he's just hungry is all. Have you had anything to eat? Maybe you would like to join us?"

Jim rose from the chair, walked toward us, and reached his arms out to shake Dominique's hand, which now shook as if Dominique had seen a ghost.

"I...I, I've got dinner waiting at home. As a matter of fact, if I don't get back right away, my wife will just—" He gulped and moved to the door. "She'll kill me. Better her than him. Bye."

With that, he dashed out the door before Jim could even say hello properly. Some people are so rude. Jim's shoulders drooped.

"Honey, don't worry about him. I know the kids will be just dying to see you." I smiled. "Well, not literally you understand, just a figure of speech."

He shrugged stiffly.

I wagged a finger at him. "No eating the kids either. The kids and I, we're off limits."

He drooped his head.

"Don't worry. There has to be some group of people who don't need brains." I grabbed a few magazines, hoping for ideas. Ads for lawyers, articles on actors, and car salesman hawking their vehicles. Not to mention the models posing in every conceivable position to sell products having nothing to do with them, like motor oil.

"Nothing here. These types all need what little brains they have left." I arose and paced back and forth while he stared out the window, watching the lightening and pouring rain.

"What we need to get are people who are smart. They can spare some brains. Maybe at a college. Probably would do you good to eat smart people's brains." Then I remembered my own college days. "Forget that, dumb idea. We won't find much there."

"Huuhuhuhuuu. Hu, huhuhuuuu." He turned to stare past me with those blank eyes.

"What?"

He held up one finger and slapped it haltingly onto his arm. "Huhhh.

"Oh, one word."

He nodded, and then repeated the action.

"One syllable."

He nodded. Then proceeded to tap his foot on the floor.

"Step."

He shook his head and tapped harder.

"Dance."

"Huhhhg." He shook his head again. Then he lumberingly but deftly tap danced a quick shuffle, ending with a final toe tap and held his arms up. "Huuhuhuhhhhh. Uh, uhuhuhhhhhhh..."

"Oh, you mean taps!"

He nodded and I almost thought I saw the corner of his mouth barely move upwards into a smile.

"I know people will have to die for you to eat their brains. That's the problem, really. Not too many will like that."

He shook his head vigorously. He apparently had something else in mind.

"You mean, people who are already dead?"

He nodded and waved his arms as if I should continue down that train of thought.

"Digging up graves, that would be a lot of work for a meal." I paced the floor again. Lightening flashed through the window, thunder rumbled the windows and my brain, and the perfect idea clicked into place amongst my gray matter.

"That's it! The morgue. You can work at the morgue. An endless supply of fresh brains—a virtual all-you-can-eat buffet of brains that no one will miss."

His eyes widened, and he clapped his hands. Well, sort of. If you can call two boards being hit together, clapping.

This activity seemed to entice Fifi to have another go at him. But I stepped in the way and he crumbled before my feet. "No, Fifi. There's not enough of him to go around."

He slumped off to his sleeping pad, whining.

"Animals. Between dealing with Fifi—your dog, by the way—and the kids sucking on me like puppies in a desert, and your brain addiction; I should be working in a circus."

"Huhhhh."

So, we enrolled Jim in a school for mortuary workers. He did have a hard time with it. I had to translate his notes into something readable. It took a while, but we developed a Zombie language involving grunts and groans in various sequences.

Even our kids grew up learning Zombise. We did tend to get stares when we went out to eat. Sitting there, grunting to one another at the table.

"What shall it be today?" The waiter held up his notepad, awaiting our decisions.

"Uh, huhu, ugh, huhuguh, hu."

"He said he would like the cow heart, rare, with a side order of gizzards and livers."

"Uhhuhuhug."

"Oh, and also a bottle of your best Chianti, please."

After a few months of intensive study, he passed and worked at the local morgue. His days of putting up with cow brains ended, much to our butcher's chagrin. But what job paid as well, and included all meals free? Saved us a lot of money.

And he came home from work so happy and full. You could tell by the lilt in his walk, in how he bent his knees ever so slightly. And how he could kiss me without attempting to take a bite. A full stomach does lead to a contented zombie.

I also discovered that he was more compliant now than before he died. He would do any task I wanted, right away. Even if he watched the game, he didn't mind breaking away to take out the garbage or take Jake and Jill to the playground.

Come to find out, having a zombie for a husband wasn't such a bad idea. As a matter of fact, he seemed more alive to me than he did then.

"I love you, Honey," I said as we sat on the porch swing, hand in rotting hand, listening to life pass us by. I gave him a kiss on the cheek.

"Uhhhhhhhh!"

Lady of the Lake Employment Office

"Do these people really think they'll be king?" John and his friend stopped at the lake's edge. A crowd of town folk mumbled on the lake's shore; many camped in tents and roasted meals over a fire.

"No," Henry said, "just the lucky peasant who catches a sword thrown by the Lady of the Lake."

"How many kings do they think England can hold?" John asked. The Lady had already given a sword to a boy named Arthur the day before. News of the give-a-way had created the current sword-seeking craze.

"There's room for a couple more kings I suspect. Too much land for one king to oversee."

"You'd think someone reported catching a record size fish." John smiled at the thought of tossing in a line but figured the crowd would burn him at the stake as a heretic if he tried.

"What do you have against becoming king anyway?" Henry looked at John from the corner of his eyes.

"Nothing really, but it's crazy to act as if the Lady will hand out swords right and left to make people king. Besides, I'm perfectly happy working with horses."

"Horses?" Henry jerked his head around to face John.

"Yea, four-legged beast you can ride. Ever heard of them?"

John felt a sting as Henry's hand landed on the back of his head.

"No," Henry said, "I mean, why are you content to work with horses over being a king?"

"Everyone is a king's judge and jury. Unless he's willing to kill people who don't agree with him." John shivered at the thought. "I'm not willing, so I'd make a terrible king." John looked at Henry and smiled. "Besides, horses don't talk back. At least usually they don't."

"Well, I don't know about you, but if the Lady appears and tosses out a sword, you can bet I'll be jumping for it." Henry rubbed his hands together in anticipation.

"Careful, catch a sword on the wrong end and you'll cut off your hand."

Henry cast a frown at John. They stood in silence.

"I need to get out of here," John said with a sudden edge. He felt too closed in by the crowd.

"I'm staying. I'll see you later at the pub," Henry said without looking.

John turned to walk, but paused. He spun back to face the lake.

"You know why the Lady hasn't come back to toss out any swords?" John asked.

"No. Why?" Henry said with a note of fear in his voice.

"She's out of swords. She doesn't have any more to give out."

"Now, that's not funny."

"I'm not trying to be funny."

John drew his sword and before Henry could stop him, he tossed it over the lake with a loud grunt. The crowd hushed and heads turned as the sword splashed water up and out over the surface of the lake. Henry's eyes grew twice their size and he backed away.

As the ripples died off, the mass of people in hushed anticipation focused their attention on John and the lake. John turned to go back to town. The sound of water splashing didn't cause him to turn but the air whooshing against his leg as a sword lodged itself into the ground caused a sudden rush of fear. He froze.

John turned to see a woman, glowing in the broad daylight as if it were night and floating on the surface of the lake.

An angelic voice echoed across the water, "Yes John, I did need another sword."

John pulled the sword out of the ground with little effort. Holding it up he said, "I suppose this means I'm to be king?"

"No, it means you're to keep the paths clear of brush in the forest for travelers."

"You want me to do what?" John said, his eyes widening.

"Clear the brush from the roads. Don't you understand?"

"What about being king?" John suddenly thought the idea of being king wasn't as bad when compared to this job.

"King? You said it yourself. I gave that job out yesterday. Now I'm giving out other more important jobs."

John looked around. There were very few sword-seekers left standing at the water's edge.

Self-Talk

I talk to myself. Does that mean I'm freaking crazy? No. It just means there's two of me.

I claim I'm from an alternate reality, a parallel universe. Like, I crossed through some portal. Maybe the bathroom. And now I'm stuck with me.

At least, that's my story. I don't know whether to trust me. I never have before. Why start now?

"When is George coming over? I'm bored."

"You keep your hot little hands off him. He's my boyfriend, girl."

"Just as much mine as he is yours."

I narrow my eyes. "Who came into whose world? Go find your own freaking boyfriend."

"Like, I'm you. How can I get a different one? We'll have to take turns."

"Share?" The nerve of me.

"Tell him the truth. If he can't accept me as I am, let him walk."

"Duh! He's not Mormon, you know."

"Like, I didn't know that? He marries one, he gets two. What guy wouldn't think that rocks?"

Barf that. I'm not biting.

"I heard that." I frowned at me.

"Time for one of us to bite the dust."

"Girl, don't make me hurt me."

The doorbell rang.

"George. Come in. I've been, like, so ready to squeeze you."

He smiled, but glanced to the side. "Uh, I have my twin brother with me."

"A twin?" I craned my neck as he slid into view.

"Yeah." His laugh stumbled over itself. "You could say, we're like the same person."

"What a rad coincidence. My twin's here too."

He nodded his head at his twin. "He demanded to come. Wanted to meet you." They walked in. "So, where's your twin?"

I smiled as I stepped away. "Um, I've got to go to the bathroom."

"Is she in there? Bogus!"

The other twin finally spoke up. "Bathroom?" He shot past me toward the door. "I need the bathroom, like, yesterday."

"But..." I raised my hand as he shut the door behind him. Soon the sounds of water flushing down a hole and the tank refilling echoed through the room.

George draped an arm over my shoulder. "Awesome. Now we're finally alone together. I thought he'd never leave."

"Right. Awesome," I echoed. "We all have to go sometime."

"Whoa! That's deep."

"You'll never know." An incompleteness filled my soul, creating a longing and desire I didn't expect. I had to go find myself. "Make yourself comfortable. I've got to go to the bathroom."

He plopped on the couch. "Isn't it getting crowded in there? Like, how many toilets you have in your bathroom?"

"Just one." I paused at the doorway and turned to George. "I need to chat with my twin. I've been giving her crap for years. About time I made peace with her."

He nodded slowly and stared at the coffee table. Then he jerked his head up. "Sounds like that could take a while. You have any beers?"

I sighed. "In the freakin' fridge."

I shut the door, and then flushed. "Hey me, it's me again."

Public Identities

Dr. Jenkins glanced at the patient and noticed his eyes flickering open. A grimace spread across the man's face as he adjusted to the light.

"Nurse, bring more covers. I don't want this patient going into shock." Dr. Jenkins felt the patient's forehead.

The man, still in a green, spandex suit and yellow cape, groaned. His eyes widened, and he jerked his hands to the top of his head. "Where's my mask?" The words left his lips as if he had to push them out.

"It is safe, Mr. McDeal."

"But my secret identity! I can't have that in the hospital records."

"Sorry, Mr. McDeal, but there is no modesty in a hospital. No secrets." Dr. Jenkins shook his head. Priorities, why can't people focus on what's important.

"But, if Zinger find out—"

"So what, if he find out? Are you going to stop being a superhero just because this Zinger knows who you are?"

The man gritted his teeth. "My loved ones, they will suffer. Zinger will attack my loved ones. That's why I wear a mask and keep a secret identity."

"And why should you be any different from all the good cops out there? The people they put in prison know who they are."

The man rolled his eyes and then glared at him. He remained silent. Either he didn't have an answer or his anger raged too hotly.

Dr. Jenkins thought he better calm the patient down, if possible. Anger hindered recuperation.

"Mr. McDeal, what is your superhero name?"

"You mean, you don't know!" His jaw dropped.

"No, I'm afraid not. I have little time to keep up with crime fighting news."

He grimaced from some hidden pain. "I'm Tornado Man."

"Tornado Man. Hum, catchy. So, what are your powers?"

"I can whip up a pretty good storm, when I need to. Lots of wind, up to 500 mph."

"And I take it this bullet wound is one your wind didn't catch?"

Tornado Man frowned. "Some new weapon Zinger shot at me, could penetrate my wind shields." He stared at Dr. Jenkins. "He's always inventing ways to get through whatever defenses I put up. He's like some freakin' computer virus."

Tornado Man's eyes widened and a grin appeared. "Of course, if you refuse to keep my name out of the records, I'll have to send a tornado to wipe out this facility."

Dr. Jenkins leaned over his bed and glared at the superhero. "I come back to my question. Why the secret identity? It makes no sense."

Tornado Man lay in bed, grumbling under his breath.

Dr. Jenkins arose, grabbed the chart at the end of the bed. He moved to the window as he studied it.

"Mr. McDeal, could your need to have a secret identity arise from self-inferiority? In real life, you don't feel important, but as a superhero, people look up to you." Dr. Jenkins turned to face Tornado Man, who stared at the ceiling. "Could it be this whole superhero gig is to compensate for the need to be somebody?"

"You don't know me." He snarled the words out. "This is no time to play physiatrist. My enemy has free reign over the city as long as I'm in here." He lifted himself to a sitting position. His head wavered.

Dr. Jenkins slipped under him as he sank to the floor. "This is no time for heroics, Mr. McDeal. I'm afraid Zinger will have some time to ransack the city before you are ready to go out again."

"Then we're doomed." He grimaced as he lay back down. "We're all doomed."

Dr. Jenkins shook his head. "Perhaps it will help to take your mind off it all." He reached for the remote and turned on the TV. The five-o'clock news popped onto the screen.

"And now for today's breaking news. Zinger, the long time rival of Tornado Man, died today while surrounded by the police. He claimed to have killed Tornado Man with a new weapon. In the process of robbing a bank, a security officer shot Zinger in the back, his one vulnerable spot. Before he lost consciousness, he said, "A freakin' bullet! All this time I planned for storms, and I get hit with a bullet."

The TV cut off; Mr. McDeal's hands shook the remote. "I'm doomed. I'm nobody again."

"Isn't that enough, Mr. McDeal?" Dr. Jenkins shook his head while staring out the window at the busy city below. "Besides, I bet you could make a killing in the demolition business."

Marvelous Man

Jared heard the door to his room fling open. He jerked his head around to see his mom walking in.

"Your dad will be up shortly to say goodnight."

Jared winced. Why did she insist on calling him his dad? "My dad isn't living here anymore. Remember?"

She started to say something, but backed off. Instead she said, "Just get ready for bed." The door clicked shut behind her.

Jared could hear the stair-steps creaking as she descended. His shoulders slumped. He had to finish his math homework first. He sat at his desk.

Jared tapped his pencil on the desktop and stared at his paper. One half-finished math problem covered the top left corner under his name. He found it difficult to focus over the feeling that the world had collapsed around him.

If Marvelous Man existed, he could save us, he would make things right.

Jared reached into his desk and pulled out a three-ring binder. On the cover he had inscribed with a marker the words, "Jared's Comics." Several stories filled its pages since he had created the character when he was six. Now, another storyline nudged its way into his consciousness; he had to draw it.

Marvelous Man streaked across the sky in red and blue tights accented with a white cape. He eyed the city below. Everything seemed quiet this evening over the Big City, but he knew better.

No sooner had the thought crossed his mind than his super radar senses detected breaking windows and an alarm sounding in the business district. He banked and plunged downward to the location. In a few seconds, his feet landed on the blacktop in front of the store.

Shards of glass littered the sidewalk. Through a hole in the plate glass window, a stream of electronics flowed into the rear of an SUV. No one seemed to notice the presence of the hero.

"You boys need some new toys?" Marvelous Man put his hands on his hips.

Everyone froze. Heads turned. One of the thieves said in a high-pitched mock, "Oh no, it's Marvelous Man. What are we going to do?" Several laughed.

Marvelous Man shook his head. *Time to take action.* He stepped toward them with gritted teeth.

Several pulled out pistols; bullets ricocheted off his chest and arms.

This will be over quick.

"Jared," Mom yelled from downstairs, "Why isn't your light off."

Jared opened the door to his attic room. "I'm doing my homework."

"You have five minutes to finish, then I'm sending your Dad to help you."

Jared slammed the door shut. A marriage and two weeks doesn't qualify anyone to replace his dad. Dealing with life at thirteen sucked enough. Then to be told, "Oh, you're getting a new dad. Your old one is leaving," had tossed his world into chaos. The whole idea blew his mind.

He sat at his desk. The last frame he had drawn needed one more item: bullets. He needed to draw bullets bouncing off the chest.

Marvelous Man didn't slow with the pulse of the bullets pelting him. As he drew near, one of the thieves popped out from behind the SUV and dropped a weapon over the hood. Its metal surface shone in the moonlight like brass and silver. The main barrel, a cylinder tapered at both ends, supported two smaller cylinders of the same shape. They glowed an alternating purple and white.

"You see, Marvelous Man, we already have toys. But this toy's for you."

"If you think a mere bullet will stop—"

The man pulled the trigger and a purple ray erupted from the gun and plowed into Marvelous Man's gut. Searing pain threw him to the ground.

The young man stepped from behind the SUV, keeping the point of the gun on Marvelous Man. "We know your weakness, Mr.

Superhero." He opened the top cylinder and pulled out a shiny piece of metal. "Aluminum."

Jared shook his head and erased the last line of dialog.

That's stupid. Besides, it's too much like kryptonite. Needs something more original.

He closed his eyes and bounced the pencil eraser off the top of his head. Five seconds passed. Then he sat up straight, his eyes sprang open, and he put pencil to paper again.

The young hooded man came from behind the SUV, keeping the point of the gun on Marvelous Man. "We know your weakness, Mr. Superhero. Like anyone else, self-doubt will paralyze you." He patted the ray gun. "This baby can infuse any emotion I want in you."

Marvelous Man felt the truth. He didn't think he could do anything right. A nagging voice in his head countered each thought to take action. He felt stupid, and could not outsmart these brilliant thieves. So he lay groveling on the ground.

Jared heard the steps creaking. Someone approached his "secret" lair. He grabbed his notebook and stuffed it back in his drawer. Then straightened out his math papers and started writing.

A knock rapped on the door and it squeaked open. The man who had recently intruded on his family life entered into the room. His balding head and moustache caused Jared to wonder what his Mom saw in him. Jared felt a knot develop in his stomach.

"Time to..." He loosened his collar. "...to turn out the lights and go to bed." He stood there, waiting for something.

Finally Jared said, "Yes, sir." Jared stared at him.

He stared back for a second. "Like, right now."

Jared slammed his math book closed and prepared for bed. Soon, his lights snapped out and the intruder left.

Jared lay gazing out the window into a star-filled night. Little wisps of clouds obscured a cluster of stars here and there.

Why did he have to go to bed so early? Many of his friends could stay up later. But Mom still treated him like a kid. Besides, how could he leave Marvelous Man in the middle of a mess?

He arose from bed, turned on the lamp at his desk, and pulled his binder out. Pencil in hand, he continued the story.

The gang of thieves piled in the vehicle while Marvelous Man lay helpless on the ground. The SUV sped away; tires screeched around a corner.

How long do these effects last?

He didn't have time to find out. Someone had funded the thieves with serious money. They had expected him.

But how can I catch them?

He shook his head, as if he could throw these feelings aside. He had to force himself, by sheer will power, to overcome the doubts that pounded in his heart and mind. He struggled to his feet.

"No, if I can't deal with these punks, then how come I can—fly!"

He leapt into the air. His hair flapped in the wind as he raced over the buildings. The knot in his stomach unwound. His quivering lips formed into a solid smile.

Jared stopped. At thirteen, fear trailed him like a bloodhound. Hair grew all over him now. He worried it might not stop and he would become an ape. He felt he existed in a no-man's land. No longer a kid but not a teen either. And now, life had ripped his dad from him. Just weekend visits remained of the relationship.

He paced the floor, then stood by the window. It opened onto the roof overlooking the front yard. A bird flew by. Jared watched it perch on a tree limb, chirp for a moment, then in a flash it disappeared into the night.

He opened the window and wind gusted in. He often visited the roof. He could sit out there for hours and watch the world go by. No one noticed him up there. It was his private perch.

Should I do this? What if someone saw?

Jared stared at the roof. It had been years since he played superhero. But now, he wanted to live in that world, even if for a moment. He wanted to conquer his fears like Marvelous Man.

Jared took off his pajama bottoms, leaving on his shirt and briefs. He grabbed a towel, threw it over his shoulders and tied it into a knot around his neck.

"I'm Marvelous Man," he said under his breath, "and I can fly."

He stepped onto the roof. The air, warm from the hot September day, blew across his bare legs and gently flapped the "cape" around him. He scooted to the edge of the roof and stood. As he surveyed the street below, a surge of excitement shot through him. Evildoers had better watch out. He was on the job.

He lifted his arms into the sky. A gust of wind caressed his skin. He closed his eyes. In his mind, he rode above cotton-like clouds accented by moonlight. Birds cried their songs as he flew by. He waved to the passengers in a jet. He could tackle problems and win: he was Marvelous Man.

Then a strong wind blew the opposite direction. Jared opened his eyes and swung his arms in an attempt to regain his balance, but he lost the battle. His cape flapped around his face as he tumbled through the air. He let out a loud cry when he landed on the lawn, bottom first. He bounced onto his back and lay groaning in the grass.

Then he heard giggles. A group of girls strolled down the sidewalk. He recognized some of them from middle school. His fingers clawed at the grass. He wanted nothing more than to dig a hole and crawl in it.

"Look! Is it a plane? Is it a train? No, it's Superboy! He can fall from roof tops in a single bound." The girls all giggled while they gawked and then continued down the street.

Now he wished he could fly away, but he felt too much pain to even get up. His embarrassing story would spread over the whole school. He laid his head back on the ground.

The porch light lit up the yard and the man who had invaded his family ran to where Jared lay. He paused when he came close enough to see Jared's "costume."

He seemed to suppress a laugh as he talked. "Jared, are you all right? Did you break anything?"

Jared kept his eyes fixed on the stars. "No and no."

The intruder sat next to him. Jared wanted to crawl away.

After the man checked Jared for damage, he said, "Just bruised up, I guess." He even sounded like he cared. "You know, I used to play around the house in my underwear and a towel around my neck too, when I was young. Unfortunately, I'm too old now or I would join you. People would get the wrong impression."

Jared cracked a smile. The image of this bald-headed man jumping around the house in underwear and a cape struck him as something off a crazy movie.

"Jared," he said with a hint of quiver in his voice, "Your Mom, she means well. But I know it's not a good idea to force you to call me 'Dad.'"

Jared looked at the man.

"It's okay to call me 'Henry.' I know I can't replace your dad any more than you can replace my sons." Henry locked onto Jared's eyes. "But that doesn't mean we can't get to know each other, in time."

Jared felt a sigh leave him. Not a sigh of frustration or dissatisfaction, but as if a weight had been lifted off his soul. He rose to a sitting position. "Sure, Henry."

Henry stood up and stretched out his hand. Jared stared at the hand. He grasped it and Henry pulled him to his feet. Pain shot through his body but his legs could move. Jared leaned on him as Henry led him into the house, up the steps, and into the attic room. Jared snuggled under the covers of his bed.

"And, let's lay off the flying lessons for now. Okay?" He smiled and shut the door.

He still had problems, but he felt a confidence not there before. Flying did help.

He arose from bed with a grimace, and turned his lamp on. He couldn't go to sleep until he finished the story.

Marvelous Man spotted the speeding SUV in his mind's radar. He dove to intercept.

He swooped over the vehicle and lifted it off the pavement. They jumped in their seats, but wasted no time before the ray gun swung out the window and a blast hit Marvelous Man on the shoulder. He forced himself to keep a grip on the vehicle through the pain.

Serenity flooded his mind and body. He no longer had a care in the world. All desire for strife and hate left him. But he couldn't let go, or these poor unfortunate victims of circumstances would plummet to their deaths. No, better to set them down at the police station where they could get the help they needed.

"You shot him with peace?" A voice said from the vehicle. "This isn't the sixties, stupid."

"If he felt peace, he wouldn't fight us."

"Does it look like he is fighting us, you idiot?"

Marvelous Man heard fists hitting heads. He wanted to stop the fighting, but holding the SUV prevented him from helping. The ray blasted inside the vehicle a couple times.

"No, no, please don't hurt me!" A voice shrieked.

"How dare you tell me what to do! I'll show you..."

Marvelous Man shook his head as he set them in front of the police station. He reached in and took the ray gun lying on the dash. The thief had dropped it in his rage.

"You boys need to lighten up." He dialed the gun and shot each with a blast. Screams and fighting turned to laughter.

"Oh, look," one said, trying to catch his breath between air sucking cries of joy, "We're going to jail." He doubled over, his face red.

Another paused from his joviality long enough to blurt out, "Curse you, Marvelous Man." He threw himself back on the seat. Sounds of eerie laughter echoed in the streets.

"That's better. Now we're all one big happy family. Enjoy your stay in the pen, fellas." Marvelous Man sprang into the air and sped off to his secret laboratory to test the gun.

The end.

Jared huddled with the rest of the football team on the field. The crowd in the stands echoed the words of the cheerleaders who bounced around, pompoms shooting up and down in rhythm.

The quarterback gave the play. The team clapped hands as they broke huddle. The crowd roared as the players lined up. Thirty yards and three seconds separated them from the end zone, the winning touchdown, and the state championship.

Jared stood in the wide receiver's slot. He glanced into the stands. Henry stood and pumped his fist into the air. He recalled that night when their relationship had turned around. He was thirteen then. Much had changed in five years.

The quarterback yelled the count and took the snap. Jared sprang forward. As he approached the defender, he faked a move to the inside. The boy fell for it and Jared cut around him.

The air flowed through his helmet as he raced down the sidelines. A check over his shoulder confirmed the ball sped to intercept him. Sweat ran down his cheeks, cooling his face. Two defenders trailed on his heel. Jared read their body language; they intended to intercept.

Jared focused. The ball flew high. He pumped his legs harder. The roar of the crowd solidified into a chant, resounding through the stadium: "Sup-er-boy, Sup-er-boy, Sup-er-boy," and it continued, ringing in Jared's ears.

The ball spiraled down. The defender next to him leaped in front but Jared knew he didn't have the reach to snag the ball.

Jared pushed himself into the air at the one-yard line. He reached out as the wind whipped around him. The moment hung in slow motion: his outstretched hands, the ball sinking, the opponent sliding under him. It bounced on his fingertips for a second, then fell into his palms.

He latched onto the ball, clutched it to his chest, landed in the end zone on his bottom, and bounced onto his back. His teammates gathered over him, jumping around like wild hyenas.

The crowd roared, but the chant continued, "Sup-er-boy, Sup-er-boy," for several minutes. The team lifted him off the ground and placed him on their shoulders.

Yes, at times Jared felt he could fly. "Thank you, Marvelous Man," he whispered.

The Carpool

Henry pulled to a stop in front of Jerry's house to pick up his new carpool partner. No one flew out the door. "He's going to make me late!" Henry slammed on the horn.

The door flung open, and Jerry rushed down the driveway, one shoe off and a loose tie flapping in the wind behind him, while trying to eat a breakfast bar.

Henry shook his head as he watched Jerry fling his briefcase into the back seat and flop down beside him, scattering crumbs around as he pulled the door shut.

"Bogus! My alarm clock didn't go off this morning."

"You're going to clean up all those crumbs, aren't you?"

"Oh, wow Dude, didn't realize I had cratered your wheels." He dusted more crumbs off his shirt and onto the floorboard.

Henry gritted his teeth. Why he had ever agreed to the carpool idea now escaped him. Yeah, at the time saving the environment sounded like a good idea, but at the expense of his sanity?

After a brief drive to the freeway, he landed in the morning rush hour traffic headed downtown. More like the morning still hour traffic, because they didn't go very fast. Reminded him of the Army: rush to stand in line. At least there you didn't have to smell everyone's gas fumes. Only an occasional rear venting.

Jerry swallowed the last of his breakfast bar and dusted the remaining crumbs into his lap. "You know what you need?"

"No, what?" Henry kept his eyes on the car in front of him to watch a movie on their TV screen.

"What you need is a set of saws on the front of this chariot, and like, you could mow your way through all this traffic."

"Saws? What are you talking about?"

"They have those now. I saw it in the movie theater. Speed Racer uses them." He stared at me as if serious.

"Ah, that's a movie. Not real life. They don't really have cars like that. Besides, even if I had such saws, I'd be put away for life if I killed all the people in front of me just so I could get to work faster."

"Whoa, Dude. I hadn't thought about that. After all, who wants to get to work faster."

Henry wrinkled his brow and stared at the man. "Who hired you?"

A grin spread across his face. "My Uncle. He's rad."

"Of course. I should have known."

"Why? Are you psychic?"

"No you crazy—"

"Oh, oh, I know! You need those legs that pop out and shoot your car into the air so you can jump over everyone. That'd be awesome!"

Henry rolled his eyes, and kept them there. "Aside from the damage such a device would do to your car upon crashing back onto the pavement, when you're sitting still, all it would do is make your car jump up and down in one place!"

"Whoa! You're right!" A silly grin danced upon his face. "You're pretty smart."

"Wish I could return the compliment." Using saw blades to shorten this ride grew more appealing by the minute. The crowd of vehicles moved forward a couple feet.

Jerry scanned the area. "Dude, we're gonna be here for a while. What if we—"

"No! No more crazy ideas. Nada, zip. Got it?"

"But I wanted—"

Henry grabbed Jerry's lips and squished them shut. "What did I just say? Did I stutter? Was I not clear enough?"

He yanked his head back out of Henry's grasp. "But if—"

"You see this button right here?" Henry pointed at the radio volume dial.

Jerry nodded.

"If you don't shut up, I'll push that button, and you'll be ejected from this car. Remember that from the movie?"

His eyes grew wide. "You..." He stopped himself short. His eyes glanced at the button, then back to Henry. He settled back in his seat and stared out the window.

Henry smiled. At last, some peace and quiet.

For a few moments, only the sounds of car horns and a street crew hammering pavement into pieces off in the distance pierced the blessed quietness in the vehicle. The line moved forward another couple feet.

Jerry dug in his pocket, then pulled out...nothing? But he held it as if it were keys. He then grabbed an imaginary steering wheel and proceeded to "start" the car.

Henry groaned. Now he's going to mime all the way to work!

Jerry flipped an imaginary turn signal switch and made a noise with his mouth, "Click, clunk, click, clunk," and spun the air-wheel to the right.

Henry's eyes followed his movements to a street leading off to the right. The construction blocking the back-road route to work had been opened after months of being closed.

"Oh look, the road's open now. Great!"

"That's what I was trying to tell you, Dude!" His eyebrows shot up. He threw his hands over the radio volume knob and waited for Henry to act.

Henry sighed. "I'm not going to eject you."

Jerry relaxed. "That's awesome, cause otherwise, I'd had to take drastic measures."

Henry laughed. "And what would that be?"

He whipped out a handle, flipped a switch, and a beam of light extended six feet from the base, searing a hole through the roof of the car. Jerry swung it around. It crackled through the metal with a hum, and a chunk of ceiling crashed between them.

Henry jumped back and gazed forlornly at his car's ceiling. "What the...!" He had created an instant sunroof. Jagged metal surrounded the hole as the light-saber hummed, throwing sparks when it bounced off the edges of the ever-widening hole.

"Where on earth did you get that?"

"Dude, from the movie, where else? Now, about those saw blades...."

The Peasant's Rule

"Look, a shiny coin," Richard said, reaching to pick it up. Sunlight sparkled off its wet surface from the dew-laden grass. "I think it's made of gold."

Henry, running up behind him, halted and peered over Richard's shoulder. "Oh, that's a really nice coin. Can I have it?"

Richard squeezed his hand shut. "No! Most certainly not. I found it, I get to keep it."

Henry's eyes widened and he stepped back. "I'm just teasing you, no need to turn on me." Henry scowled while flipping his shoulder-length, brown hair back. "Besides, I doubt it's worth much. Probably why it ended up on the side of the road."

Richard shoved it in his pocket. It might at least buy some food for him and his father. They resumed their walk to the city gate, passing by fields of sparse wheat stalks. "How do you know this coin isn't magical? I bet I can wish for something and it'll happen."

"That's just superstitious nonsense. Besides, what useful thing would a fourteen-year-old boy like you wish for? Probably a wagon full of rock candy to get sick on!" Henry chuckled.

"I'll have you know, this fourteen-year-old boy has more sense than that." He held his nose up in the air in mock offence.

"I know. You'll wish for a wagon of gold so you can buy yourself all the rock candy you can get!" Henry slowed his walking as he laughed.

"I'm not that bad!" Richard swatted Henry on the back of the head. "No, what I would wish for is to be king."

"King?" A couple more heaves left Henry's throat as he fought to control the laughter. "So you can command that all taxes be paid in rock candy!"

Laughter broke forth from Henry once again. Richard tackled him and they both rolled off the side of the road, soaking their clothes in the morning dew. After a minute of play fighting, they lay on their backs smiling at the clouded sky.

After Richard caught his breath, he turned to Henry, his smile dimming. "No, if I were king, I would fix all the problems. Like my father. He struggles to put food on the table. Yet, the king taxes him, making it hard to provide for us. I would take care of my father and others like him."

Henry rose to his feet and helped Richard to his. "Such noble words coming from a fourteen-year-old peasant. I bet if you did become king, you'd find out it's not easy."

Richard brushed grass off his clothes as they resumed their progress to the city gate. "Maybe, but still, if I had a wish, I would wish to be king, even for a day. Then I would fix things around here so everyone would be happier."

"Some people say, take heed to wishes. They can come true," an unfamiliar deep voice sounded from behind Richard.

Richard spun around; his heart skipped a beat. A man of about five and a half feet sat upon a proud black steed. His black cloak flowed over the saddle, and though his hood lay behind his back, his long black hair blended with his cloak as if part of it. What caught Richard's attention were his eyes. They looked old, experienced, but hidden as if some dark secret lay behind them.

The stranger continued, "A wish is a risky thing. Don't wish lightly, my child." His voice felt commanding and weighty.

Richard and Henry bowed before him, "Thank you kind sir for your words of wisdom," Richard said, not taking his eyes off the man.

He nodded and shook the reigns in his hand. His horse trotted through the city's gates and disappeared into the crowd as he rounded a corner.

"Weird," Henry broke the silence as they stared after him. "He gave me the creeps."

"Yeah, me too." Even though the stranger had warned him, yet, it still seemed a good idea to Richard. After all, his parents named him after a great king. Why shouldn't he be king?

They soon resumed their stories and jokes as they finished walking through the fields and entered into the city gates.

———

A solid rapping noise rang in Richard's ears. He pulled the covers over his head. On his one day to sleep in, why did his father attempt to wake him?

A louder rap on the door drove him more fully awake. The rapping sounded strange to Richard. It didn't sound like the tone of his door. He rubbed the cloth between his fingers; it felt silky. One feeling was absent, the persistent feeling of hunger that always gnawed at his stomach.

He pulled the covers off his head and forced his eyes to open. Was he dreaming? It seemed real enough. Yet, this wasn't his room. A marble-topped dresser, a seven-foot mirror, and beautifully gold inlaid chairs adorned the room. He lay in a canopied bed with silk covers and a feather mattress. He had never felt a bed so rich and soft.

Richard gaped at his surroundings, ignoring the continuing rapping on the door.

Finally, the door cracked open and a man stuck his baldhead into the room. "Sire, I'm sorry to move you along, but you're meeting with your advisor and then the counts. The time will soon be upon you if you do not arise and prepare."

"Excuse me, but who are you?" Richard started to get up, but thought he might not be properly clothed, so stayed under the covers.

"I see you are having trouble waking up this morning, Sire. At least you are up. I would suggest you get moving, at your leave of course. We have a busy day today." His head disappeared and the door closed with a thud.

Did he say "Sire?" What is going on here? Where am I? Richard slipped out from under the covers. He felt silk pajamas brushing against his body. Seeing a window, he walked to it and looked out, hoping to see anything familiar.

Richard widened his eyes in astonishment. He was still in town, but judging from the streets below, he stood in the king's castle. But how? Why? He dropped his head, trying to figure it out.

He stared at his hands absently but then focused on them. His heart skipped a beat and his mouth fell open. These were not his hands. Richard dashed to the mirror, almost stumbling before he reached it.

The king's wrinkled face, curly hair and brown eyes stared back at him. He staggered backwards at the sight, as if some strange man had entered the room. This didn't make any sense. He sat down in a nearby chair before his knees, now shaking, gave way. He sank his head into the king's hands.

Then he remembered. "I wish I were king," he had said. He had joked about the coin being magical, but the man had acted as if it were serious. Could the coin really have been magical? How else to explain all this?

Richard thrust his hand into his left pocket, the one in which he had put the coin. He pulled his hand out; the shiny gold coin rested between his fingers. He stared at it for a long minute.

His heart rate increased, small beads of sweat broke upon his now aged brow. I have to undo this. "I wish…"

Another loud rap at the hardwood door interrupted his words. "Sire." The baldheaded man had cracked the door open. "I do hope you are ready. There are only a few minutes before your first meeting. Already you will have to eat breakfast while you meet with your advisor."

"I'll be right there, just tell my advisor to wait."

"Ay, Sire." The door shut again.

Richard realized even if he wished again, it probably wouldn't change him back right away. Besides, he did wish to become king. Now that it had actually happened, maybe he should take advantage of it. After all, it isn't every day you get to be king.

He arose from his chair and placed the coin on the dresser. Opening a door, he discovered a long hallway lined with clothing. "How do I choose from all this?" He didn't have time to worry about it. He grabbed the closest thing he could find: a set of puff-out pants with gold and red stripes running their length, a blue shirt with a lacy collar, and a golden, knee-length robe. He struggled to figure out how to put it on. In a few moments, he stood dressed before the mirror, correctly he hoped.

He scanned the dresser. On it lay a crown. Constructed of gold, red gems topped each of its twelve points around its crest. One point rose higher than the others, adorned with a one-inch emerald of radiant green. Richard picked it up. Standing in front of the mirror, he placed it on his head and threw his shoulders back. "I am now King Anthony Hawthorn, king of all Noland." Richard cracked a smile. "At least for a day." Maybe this would be fun after all.

He started to walk towards the door, but stopped. He turned and reached to retrieve the coin off the dresser. *Don't want to forget this, it's my way back home when I'm done here.*

As he walked to the door, tucking the coin in a pocket, a thought surfaced. *I don't know anyone's names? I hope I can fake it well enough.* He opened the door and walked into the hall.

Richard noticed this body moved more reluctantly than his own. The joints rebelled as he walked down the hall. No wonder the king always seemed so stiff.

The hall ended at the intersection of another hall. *Do I go right or left?* As he contemplated, a servant girl walked past with a tray of food. "My fair lady, that wouldn't be my breakfast would it?"

She stopped, curtsied while carefully balancing the tray in her hands. "Why yes Sire, it is. Would you rather have it in your dining room?"

"No, no. I'm meeting with...my advisor. I'll have it with him. I mean, in his room." Richard nervously smoothed out the wrinkles on his shirt. He hoped he seemed natural but he felt stupid.

"As you wish, Sire." She proceeded down the hall after giving him a sideways glance.

Richard relaxed, and followed her. Her petite body, blond hair and big blue eyes captivated him. She appeared about Richard's age, at least his real body's age. He liked the way she smiled at him.

Soon they came to a heavy wooden door with a brass handle formed into the shape of a snake. As the door opened, Richard felt the color drain from his face. The man sitting at the table, his advisor, was the man he had met yesterday who said, "Be careful what you wish for."

"Don't just stand there, King Anthony. Come in before your food gets cold." He had a crooked smile on his face. He stood and bowed to Richard. His upturned mouth and squinting eyes lacked the humility a bow would normally convey.

Richard started to bow back, but caught himself. He sat down at the table as the young servant girl placed fruit, ham and goat's milk before him. He glanced at the nameless man who seemed to enjoy looking at him. He still felt creepy.

"Sir Rimal, will you require any breakfast to eat with the king?" The servant girl placed her hand on a plate in anticipation.

Ah, now I know his name. Richard stuck his fork into some ham.

"No, I've already eaten." Rimal waved his hand. She bowed and departed.

Before placing his first forkful into his mouth, Richard asked, "What news do you have for me today?"

Rimal rattled off a series of issues from skirmishes at the kingdom's border to a list of suggested new laws and modifications to existing laws. Richard pretended to be attentive, but most of the information passed over him. Rather, his hunger awoke after the first bite of ham. It had been years since he tasted ham. Richard sped up the rate of consumption.

After a couple minutes, Rimal halted his list. "Sire, you act like you haven't eaten in weeks. Are you feeling well?" Though it sounded well meaning, the slight crack of a smile indicated his amusement.

"Oh...yes...I'm..." He swallowed the food in his mouth. "...all right. It's just this ham taste delicious."

"There is one other thing then." Rimal's lips turned down. "There is a traitor we have caught. What is to be done with him?"

"A traitor?" Richard chewed for a moment before swallowing. "Who is it? What has he done?"

"He attempted to impersonate the king."

Richard froze. *That's what I'm doing. I'm committing a crime of treason. It will be my head if I'm caught.* Richard cast a nervous smile at Rimal. "Well, we can't have anyone running around doing that. How old is this traitor?"

Rimal leaned over the table, his eyes getting bigger. "He is fourteen."

Richard placed another bite in his mouth, to keep it busy and not betray his fear. This boy must be Richard's real body. If he inhabited the king's body, it could only mean the king existed in his body.

"I decree to lock him up for now. I'll decide his fate later." Richard scraped the last of the food onto his fork and stuffed it in his mouth.

"The laws you have signed state such a one should be put to death, Sire."

Richard knew he couldn't kill his own body. He didn't want to stay in the king's body forever. Besides, this morning only showed him he didn't know anything about running a country. So many heavy decisions to make.

"If I signed those laws, then you are bringing this to my attention because..."

Rimal frowned. "Because the law also says the king has to authorize a death sentence."

"Right!" Richard felt pleased for bluffing through to a solution. "In this case, I want to wait and think this over. He is so young to receive a death sentence. I will meet with him later to determine his intent and fate." Richard figured that would at least keep the real king out of the way.

Rimal leaned back in his chair, a frown of disgust creased his face. "If that is settled, it is time for you to address the people of your kingdom in court." He arose, his robes flowing as he walked to the door.

Richard pushed his plate back, gulped down the last of the milk, and arose to follow him.

Richard entered the throne room behind Rimal as trumpets sounded. He had been here a couple of times with his Father. Curious on-lookers lined the long hallway. Columns running along each side supported a high ceiling. Ornate carvings of horses and dragons decorated each column. Royal banners of reds, blues, greens, and yellows draped the walls.

Richard caressed the arm rests as he sat on the throne. He felt on top of the world, having immense power to command.

"I would like a little wine while I give judgments," Richard said. He figured he might as well take advantage of the position. As the door at the end of the hall opened, a servant handed a glass to him and he took a gulp.

"The Peasant Horatio requests an audience with your Majesty," a court caller announced.

Then silence, as all eyes stared at Richard. Everyone expected him to say something. "Well, bring him in."

Puzzled looks appeared on faces through the hall. The guards motioned for the man to enter. An aged man slowly walked to the foot of the steps and prostrated himself before the king. His tattered clothing and rough hands told a tale of hard work through many years.

"Rise peasant, ask of me what you wish." Richard thought he sounded kingly enough.

"Long live King Anthony," the man said, "and I pray you will be merciful to me. I have no money to pay the taxes. I will have to sell my land to pay them, and then I will be nothing but a poor beggar with no way to earn my living. I beg of you, have mercy, Sire." He then bowed before Richard, awaiting the judgment.

Richard rubbed his chin, thinking. "What can you afford?"

The man looked up from the ground. "I have but only five shilling to my name until the harvest brings in more, Sire."

"Then you shall owe me two shillings to satisfy your taxes for this year."

The man's face lit up, a bright grin showed his decaying teeth. "Oh Sire, you're so merciful and kind!" He bowed repeatedly until a guard took him away.

Richard felt a warm and happy glow. This is what he said he would do, help people. He glanced at Rimal, who had a disgruntled frown, his eyes narrow underneath his black and bushy eyebrows.

Visitor after visitor came to the throne. Time and again, Richard would give them what they wanted. After a couple of hours, however, Richard tired and he decided he could only do one more.

"The Lord Byron requests an audience with your Majesty."

"Bring him on in." The crowd no longer reacted to the odd change in ritual. Richard shifted in his seat, trying to steady his restless leg. He drained the rest of his wine. It helped him to relax.

Richard had seen Lord Byron in the market place before. A proud lord, he owned vast amounts of land in the kingdom and so wielded much power. He entered; a blue coat trimmed in gold and red pants added to his stately posture. Lord Byron stopped at the foot of the throne and bowed.

"My king, may you live long. I have come to ask for your aid in the punishment of certain peasants. They have burned fields and houses. Their crimes go beyond my own authority and ability, so I ask you to sentence them to death." He bowed again.

Richard wrinkled his brow. He didn't trust rich lords. He no doubt exaggerated so he could do as he wished against innocent peasants he didn't like. A lord had accused his own father with such an excuse before.

"My loyal subject, Lord Byron," Richard could feel he would enjoy this. "If we put everyone to death over such trifle matters, there would be no one else left to govern!" Richard heard a low rumble of chuckles in the crowd. "I'll have one of my craftsman fashion a paddle for you, then you can spank them yourself!" The crowd laughed and murmuring flowed in the background.

Lord Byron, however, didn't laugh. His face now burned red with anger. Despite the strained voice and clenched jaw, he maintained proper court protocol. "My king, I should not need to remind you, if these people are encouraged, they will go to further extremes. We can contain them now, but not much longer if we fail to act."

Richard looked over at Rimal. He had his head buried in his hands. These powerful and rich people all thought alike, apparently. "You may or may not be right, Lord Byron. Yet, we should not resort to death so easily. Deal with them yourself."

Richard rose from the throne. Several who had been sitting quickly scurried to their feet, caught unaware. Surprised trumpeters hurriedly announced the king's departure. Rimal followed close on the king's heels.

Rimal motioned for Richard to follow him into a room. No sooner did the door close than he started in.

"Sire..." He paused, as if unsure how to proceed. He paced back and forth over the floor rapidly. Then he turned to face Richard. "Sire, what madness has overtaken you? Why did you toss out money belonging to you by granting so many requests for relief, and meanwhile denying traitors their just punishment?"

"The kingdom's money? They worked for that money, they are giving it to us to protect them. We are not throwing money out the door by giving it to them, but letting the rightful owners keep it so they can live a decent life. We should not live off of them, but help them to live well. That's our job."

Rimal went back to pacing the floor. Then his jaw set, his eyes narrowed, and he moved into Richard's face, discarding all respect for kingly protocol.

"Look, your majesty, I know you are not King Anthony. You are just a poor peasant boy named Richard."

Richard widened his eyes in shock. *How did he know? Was I obvious? Surely not.*

He continued, "I placed the coin in your path, I endued it with magical qualities, and I switched you with the true King Anthony." He turned and paced the floor again.

Rimal's voice had taken on the same commanding weight it did yesterday, the same voice one uses to talk to those of inferior rank. Yet, something didn't make sense. "But, how did you know what I would wish for?"

"Pure coincidence. A fortunate one in some ways, but nothing I planned. You would have been switched no matter what you wished for."

"But why did you want to switch us? For what purpose?"

Rimal smiled, and his chuckle sent chills down Richard's back. "That, boy, is not something I wish to divulge to you." He then moved into Richard's face again. "I will tell you this much. You will do as I say, you will sign the laws I tell you to sign and make the judgments I judge you should. I have the authority and power to make life miserable for you and your father. If you love him, you will keep your mouth shut and only do what I demand. Is that clear?"

Richard felt trapped. He nodded yes, his only option. His little playful wish had now turned into a nightmare within four hours.

"Good. Do what I say and everything will be fine. Deviate even a little, and you will rue the day." Rimal stared into Richard's face. Then he abruptly pulled away and walked out the room.

Richard sat in his room. The rest of the day had gone without incident, but his thoughts focused on Rimal. Richard deduced Rimal's plan, even if he didn't state it. Put an easy-to-control peasant boy in place of the king, have the real king killed as a traitor, and then Rimal would be able to rule the country as he saw fit. He must have thought he could control Richard from the background and so keep his plan hidden, but Richard's court decisions revealed his plan wouldn't work. Now Rimal had taken a more direct path.

Aside from the prospect of being under Rimal's control for the next several years of his life, Richard didn't want to stay in the king's body. He wished for a day, not a lifetime, whatever lifetime this body still had left.

Richard still had one advantage. Rimal couldn't tell anyone Richard was not the king without revealing his plot. Everyone would still treat him as such. His body, the one the real king now resided in, should still be in the prison, safe for the moment.

Richard heard a knock at the door. He had hoped he could be alone with his thoughts at the end of the day. "Does a king ever get any rest?" He arose from his chair and opened the door.

In slipped the girl he had seen earlier. This time, she carried no food. She curtsied and looked at him with her blue eyes, awaiting something.

Not knowing what else to say, Richard suggested, "Sit down." Her narrow but firm face, her blue eyes, and blond hair gave her an angelic air.

"Sire," she said, "I've been informed it is my turn."

My turn? What is she talking about? "What is your name?" Richard had to know. He didn't want to keep thinking of her as "that girl with the tray of food."

She blushed, "Sire, you have never asked me my name before."

Good, Richard thought, *I'm not supposed to know.* "And it's high time I asked." Richard waited.

She caught her breath and spoke, "Michelle, Sire."

"That's a fine name, one to be proud of."

She looked down, fiddling with the edge of her dress. Without warning, she walked to the bed and sat on the edge. Her head hung down, as if she were waiting for something.

Suddenly it dawned on Richard why she came. He sat down in the chair by the dresser. Some boys would dream of such a situation. Now faced with it, even with a beautiful girl, it felt wrong. Even if the king and Michelle had done this before, he couldn't bring himself to do it now. It felt too much like using her, and no woman deserved such humiliation. Richard could already see it written on her face as she awaited his advance.

Then an idea surfaced. "Michelle, I have an errand I wish you to run for me."

She looked up with a wrinkled brow. "An errand, Sire?"

"Yes, hold on." Richard pulled out a piece of parchment. Using a quill and a bottle of ink on the dresser, he wrote a note. Richard had learned to read and write, his father had seen to it. He finished writing the note, folded it up, put it in an envelope, sealed it and wrote the recipient's name on the outside. He then extended it to Michelle.

She arose from the bed, took it from his hands and read the outside. "Henry?"

"Yes, he lives in the second house on Oak Lane. When you hand this to him, tell him the king wishes him to appear at the king's court tomorrow to pay his family's taxes—in rock candy."

Michelle wrinkled her nose and looked up at the king, as if he had gone crazy. "Rock candy, Sire?"

"Yes, he will understand."

She stood there holding it in her hands, appearing not to know her next move.

"Go on," Richard encouraged her, "I will require nothing more from you tonight."

She walked towards the door, moving slowly as if at any minute he would change his mind.

"Oh, I do wish one more thing."

She halted, turning back towards him. Richard left his chair and stood over her. She couldn't have been more than fifteen or sixteen. He reached down and kissed her lips tenderly. They parted slowly after long seconds had passed.

She looked as entranced as Richard now felt. He knew if he had a choice, this would be his wife. Her face, however, revealed both love and revulsion. Richard figured she must endure these times with the king. Now she had actually felt something. She didn't know how to interpret such a loving kiss from one who had treated her as a tool to satisfy his lust for so long.

"You may go, Michelle, and don't delay. Get the message to him tonight."

She curtsied again. Walking backwards as she kept her eyes on Richard, she slowly moved to the door, and finally it shut behind her.

Richard changed into his nightclothes and lay on the soft, silky bed. "Tomorrow should be quite interesting."

The following day started out pretty much the same as the day before. This time, Richard awoke early. He took breakfast in his room; Michelle had brought it to him again. She assured him she had delivered the note.

He took longer to choose his clothes this morning. After dressing, he left for his day's duties. Soon, he sat listening to Rimal in the morning advisory session.

As the previous morning, Rimal droned on and on about this or that issue. Except this time, he didn't pretend Richard had any say, but told him what he would be saying and signing into law. Richard could tell, even with his limited knowledge of the kingdom's politics, many of the laws would give Rimal more power, more money or hand out favors to friends as well as punishments to enemies.

"So, boy..." He had now taken to calling him boy in private to make sure Richard understood his place. "Did you get all that? I won't tolerate deviation or your father will pay."

"Yes." Richard arose from his chair and went over to Rimal. He reached down and gave Rimal a long hug. Rimal flinched, feeling as cuddly as a tree trunk to Richard's arms. Apparently, arms rarely enclosed him.

"Your purpose in that display, boy?"

"I thought last night: I'm stuck in this situation so I might as well make the best of it. If we can be friends, maybe you will eventually trust me enough to share in this venture."

Rimal smiled, "Well, for a peasant boy, you aren't stupid. Fine, but know this," his face grew darker, "We are not friends. You are my slave, and I will treat you as one."

"If you say so. That may one day change." Richard expected it to change today. Especially since he, while hugging Rimal, had slipped the magical coin into his pocket.

After a meeting with several lords, the time arrived to hold court again. In the meetings and now as Richard settled onto the throne to see the people of the kingdom, Rimal stayed close to Richard's side, whispering the answers he should give when needed.

As the people filed in, each one asked for relief from their taxes to fixing the city walls. Hearing one complaint after another tired Richard. *Is everyone this unhappy in the kingdom? No wonder the king always seems so grouchy.*

In many of the cases, Rimal would tell him what to say. He wiped out the decrees of the previous day, even ordering the execution of his body. However, he successfully gave it a time later in the day. Rimal didn't stop him, probably figuring it wouldn't make any difference. Richard hoped it would.

Where is Henry? Richard took a gulp of his ale.

Only a few minutes passed before Henry finally arrived, carrying a bag. After being introduced and walking to the throne, he bowed. He gazed up at the king. Richard winked at him and Henry cracked a smile.

"What can I do for you, lowly peasant boy?" Richard smiled at him.

Henry narrowed his eyes, but noticing the stares of people around him, quickly changed his expression. He bowed low again, "Sire, I have come to pay my taxes."

Richard motioned for a guard to bring the bag to him. Upon receiving it, he poured a couple chunks of rock candy into his hand. Richard scowled. "Is this a joke, boy? Since when do you pay the king in rock candy?"

The shocked Henry prostrated himself before the throne. Richard hated doing this to his friend, but if his plan worked, it had to look real.

A few seconds passed, then Richard motioned for Rimal to draw closer. He whispered in Rimal's ear, "I'll give him the coin, and you switch him with whoever you wish." Richard held his breath. Would Rimal take the bait? Richard hoped Rimal's pride and Richard's cooperative attitude earlier would be enough. Rimal's face broke into a smile and he nodded.

Richard arose from his throne and walked down the steps to Henry. "Boy, I am willing to forgive you this time. I will pay you one coin for these candies. Then go, and bring back what is rightfully due me in money."

Henry wrinkled his brow, but then reached out and accepted the coin from Richard's hand. Henry bowed once again, "Thank you, Sire. I shall not forget this." He then arose and turned to walk out the doors.

Rimal pulled his hood over his head and muttered words of a spell, then lifted his arms in a final gesture. Then he froze. Henry also froze in his tracks, as if his feet had stuck to the floor. It appeared the plan had worked. Rimal had unknowingly switched himself with Henry because Rimal had the real magical coin, not Henry.

Richard pointed at Rimal, "Guards, arrest that boy. I've changed my mind, he will go to prison until his taxes are paid."

As the guards moved towards him, Rimal ran for the door. The guards easily intercepted him, quickly bound his hands, and brought Rimal back to the king. His protest, "I'm the king's advisor, let me go!" only brought laughter from the guards.

Richard looked up at Rimal's body standing beside him. Henry's face burned red with Rimal's anger, then softened to confusion.

Henry stared at his body held by the guards, then at Richard, lost and disoriented. "Why is my body down there?" Henry's softer expression looked out of place on Rimal's usually hard and commanding face.

Richard smiled. "I'll explain later my trusted councilor, Rimal."

Henry raised his hands and looked over his body with wide eyes.

Turning back to the guards, Richard commanded, "Take this boy to prison before I pronounce a worse judgment upon him." The guards complied, but didn't reach more than halfway down the room when the doors flung open. In came Lord Byron and a couple of the guards. They looked sweaty and frantic.

The chief palace guard stopped and bowed quickly to the king. "Sire, we have a revolt on our hands. The peasants, they are at the door of the castle, demanding to see you or threatening to burn it all down, and you with it."

Lord Byron could no longer hold back. "You see, Sire, with all respect, I told you this would happen. When I attempted to deal with them myself, the situation worsened. Now they have burned many houses and businesses in towns as well as crop in the fields. Hardest hit were the peasants on Oak Lane."

Both Richard and Henry froze in shock. A great desire to run out the building to his father overtook Richard. Yet, Richard knew he wouldn't get far with the mob outside the castle. Not in this body.

Richard paused in thought. Then an idea came. "Guards, go to the prison and bring out the boy accused of treason. Bring him and this one here to the front steps of the castle. I will meet you there."

The guards paused for a moment. One of them shrugged their shoulders and then they left to fulfill the king's wishes. Soon, with Henry by his side and Rimal held by the guards, Richard waited at the entrance. He could hear the chanting of the crowds outside, drowning out all other background noise.

Soon, Richard saw his thin frame, topped with black, shaggy hair, and ragged clothes, walking down the hall. He felt odd seeing his own body from the outside. Likewise, the true King Anthony stared at Richard, eyes wide in wonder.

"Let's join the crowd." Richard opened the doors and walked out.

As they came to the top of the steps, the crowd quieted down. They obviously didn't think the king would really come out. Richard heard a low rumble of murmuring.

"My dear subjects," Richard said, "I do wish to hear your demands. Do you have one who speaks for you?"

The noise level rose noticeably. Within a minute, a man broke from the sea of people to ascend the steps. "Yes, Sire, I will speak for them."

"What is it you want?"

"We need the taxes lowered. More than half our crops and cattle go to your coffers. We have little left to support ourselves, to feed our families. We are starving." The crowd rumbled louder in affirmation.

King Anthony shook Richard's head "no" quite vigorously. Richard leaned over to listen what the true king had to say.

"These people are lying to pay less, don't let them get away with it."

"No Sire," Richard whispered into what should be his ear, "I know what they say to be true. There are weeks my own father cannot eat but a few bites of bread."

Richard's true face went from hard to soft. Richard realized the king had no doubt eaten his stingy breakfast, a roll with some milk. Many breakfasts weren't even that good. He would have slept on Richard's hard bed with coarse blankets. The king could not deny the truth Richard and the other peasants spoke of. He had experienced it first hand.

"Get rid of him," came one shout from the crowd. The phrase echoed through the unstable crowd more frequently. Richard knew he needed to act quickly.

"My subjects." The crowd grew quiet again. "You are correct, the taxes are too high. I have not overseen this as closely as I should have, and my advisor here, has in his greed, raised the taxes way beyond our need."

"Don't get me killed," he heard Henry whisper.

Rimal struggled against the guards, but they held him firmly in place, Henry's weak body being no match against the guard's muscles.

Richard continued, "Yet, we do need to operate, to protect and govern the country. So neither can we do away with taxes or you may be dealing with conquering armies invading our lands and anarchy.

"Instead, as of this day, all taxes are reduced to no more than one fourth of your new crops and cattle in a given year. Is that fair?" Richard looked over the crowd. He heard a dull rumble among them.

The man went to discuss it with some of the people in the front. Soon he returned. "Sire, we are taken aback by your generosity. We have decided we will accept your offer. However, if this turns out to be a trick, we will quickly rise up again and next time there will be no pauses for negotiation."

"I understand. Be assured, I realize the need, and will respond. A happier kingdom is a happier king." Richard smiled.

The crowd gradually broke up. Richard had averted a disaster.

Richard first saw to the safety of his father and the other peasants affected by the riots. Afterwards, Richard ordered the guards to bring the two boys with him to his room, along with Henry. Once inside, he ordered the guards to leave.

Richard walked over to Rimal, stuck his hands in Rimal's pocket and pulled out a coin. He held it up to King Anthony for inspection.

"Sire, my apologies at taking your place, but I had no part in affecting it. Rimal has admitted to me he caused our switch via this coin. Apparently a magical coin. I found it two days ago. The next morning I awoke in your bedroom and body. I figured Rimal wanted to kill you as a traitor and use me, who had little knowledge of how to run a country, to take over." Richard turned to Rimal to speak but King Anthony interrupted.

"Why you low down, no good for nothing scoundrel!"

Henry backed away. "Who, me?"

"No, Sire," Richard interrupted, "that's not Rimal. Rimal resides in my friend Henry's body, over here."

King Anthony paused, then turned to Rimal. "How could I have trusted you all these years? What did I do to deserve this?"

"You sick man," Rimal jerked Henry's head around to face King Anthony. "It's not about you, it's about me. You never considered what I wanted. I wanted what you had, and I almost had it too if it hadn't been for this kid." He scowled at Richard.

Richard thought it a little strange to be watching his body and Henry's having an intense argument. Richard broke in, "Look, Rimal, the fact is, if you want to get back to your own body, you are going to tell us how to change me and the king back as well as you and Henry."

A grin appeared on Henry's face. Richard had never seen Henry's expression look that way before; chills ran down Richard's back.

Rimal spoke, "All right, give me the cloak and I'll change everyone back."

"Oh no, I'm not that stupid. You will tell us what to say and Henry here," he pointed to Rimal's body, "will do the switching."

Rimal grumbled and delayed, but eventually gave in. He instructed Henry on what to say. After putting the coin in Richard's pocket, Henry pulled the hood over his head and cast the spell.

Richard's world swirled till it looked as if he were going to black out but gradually his surroundings came into focus and the spinning slowed to a stop. He now saw the king's body outside of him. Richard took the cloak from Henry, and changed him and Rimal back to their proper bodies. Richard took the cloak off and lifted it for King Anthony to take while guards led Rimal to prison for the king to decide his fate.

King Anthony came to Richard, and knelt before him. "My dear boy, Richard, my how your father loves you. You have a great treasure there, one worth preserving."

Richard smiled broadly.

He continued, "You have saved my kingdom. I am forever in your debt. I would be most happy if you would become my new advisor, as you have outsmarted my former one. I sense you have a better moral center for the job. Keep his robe and use it well."

Richard bowed before the king, "I am honored, Sire. I would only ask one thing. I wish to take Michelle as my wife."

"Michelle?" The king looked up thinking.

"Yeah, the girl that brings food."

"Ah," a smile spread across his face, "I take it she came to you last night and you liked her."

"Yes Sire, but I didn't take her. I had her run an important errand for me. She is sweet and beautiful." Richard paused and then said, "Actually, I love her. Her humility won me over."

King Anthony looked admiringly at Richard. "I can see I have a lot to learn from you. You are wiser than the wisest person in my kingdom. You shall have her if you wish."

"Of course, I only want her if she wants me."

"Why don't you ask her yourself, she has walked in with food as we talked."

Richard briskly turned around, and then felt his face reddening with embarrassment. Michelle sat the tray of food on the table, and walked to stand in front of Richard.

"I only need to know one thing," she said. Then she grabbed Richard and kissed him; Richard's arms flailed about. Then, his arms calmed, wrapped around her, and their lips eventually parted. "Yes," she said, "I will marry you. I knew when you kissed me last night you were not the king."

They hugged while the others looked on. Henry spoke up, "Hey Richard, have any more rock candy around?"

Baby Truth

Ashley jerked her eyes awake. She nudged Michael. "Honey, I heard something, like someone stalking through the house."

He shook his head and rubbed his eyes. "Probably the dog."

"Maybe, but let's check. I want to make sure Page is okay."

They both slid out of bed and crept into the hallway. An eerie, green light emanated from around the door of Page's room. They glanced at each other, then stood on either side of the door. Michael reached over and nudged the door open.

They both peeked in. Ashley threw her hand over her mouth. Another baby, about a year old, stood in Page's crib, its hand on Page's head. A greenish glow surrounded the strange baby.

Michael flung the door open and raced in. Ashley followed close behind him. The baby jerked its head up but couldn't react before Michael grabbed it.

"Put me down," a mature but high-pitched voice said.

Ashely saw the mouth move, but the sound didn't match anything babyish.

"So, you can talk?" Michael rotated the baby around as if trying to find a hidden speaker.

"Affirmative." The baby squirmed in his hands.

"What were you doing in our baby's crib?"

"If you must know, communicating with Page."

"Communicating?" Michael raised an eyebrow. "What would Page have to talk about? She's just a baby."

"Page gathers information on this world's conditions."

Ashely eyed the baby. "This world? What do you mean?"

The baby jerked its shoulders, trying to free its hands. "Release me and I'll answer your query!"

Michael held the baby for another second and then sat it on the changing table.

"I'm from the fifth dimension, where babies come from."

Michael's eyes grew wide and he glanced at Ashley. "What do you mean, where babies come from?"

"It's simple really, though you're not likely to believe me."

Ashely cocked her head to one side. "Neither would anyone believe us if we told them we had an intelligent conversation with a one-year-old."

The baby nodded. "Point taken. The reality is, a woman's womb is a dimensional portal. The co-joining of two people unlocks the portal, allowing a baby to enter this world. For over a year, they retain the intelligence from our world, but by two-years-old, they complete the transition into your world and no longer remember ours.

"So, we make trips to gather information they have learned from your world before we lose communication with them. Your child is nearing that stage."

The baby told the truth, Ashely did have trouble believing it. Yet... "So, you've been talking to Page?"

The baby nodded its head.

"What did she say about us, then?"

The baby smiled. "That you're good parents, but you need to lay off the broccoli baby food."

Ashely met Michael's eyes. "She does spit it out."

Michael lowered his gaze to the baby's level. "So, everyone in your world is a baby?"

"Correct."

"What would happen if I went back with you?"

"You would revert back. Not immediately, but you would shift back into your baby form after a year or two."

Ashley shook her head. "No, Honey. One baby in the family is enough."

He shrugged his shoulders. "So, how are you able to get here without a womb?"

"I'm here for a few moments, at the call of Page."

"Page called you?" Ashley let her mouth fall open.

"Yes." The baby pulled a small device from the side of its diaper. "But now I must go. One last thing."

"Yes?"

"She loves you both." The baby wavered until it dissolved into a bright green light, and then it shrank as if sucked into a hole until only a pale moonlight lit the two faces staring at nothing.

They gazed into the crib. Page eyed them and smiled. The slightly upturned corners of her mouth told Ashely that Page understood they knew—as if she had been caught with her hand in the cookie jar, but had been told to go ahead and eat one anyway.

Ashley stared at Page. "I did have one other question for that baby."

"What?" Michael asked.

"I wonder, who changes their diapers?"

Shake, Rattle, and Roll

The phone rattled the air with its ringing. Jeremy sighed. It had been a long day. He thought about not answering, but a few minutes remained before closing time. The customer had to be served.

"Hello, Bandi Breads, how can I help you?"

"I need some bread, and a cake for my son's birthday party. But I hoped you could recommend one."

Jeremy let himself fall against the wall as if he held it up. Not the First Lady again! Doing a job for the President, while an honor, tended to produce a lot of stress.

"What does your son like?"

"Well, he's patriotic and likes sports."

"I've got the perfect cake. A strawberry cake, topped with slivers of strawberry and blueberries on white frosting to make a flag. Then I'll infuse it with the Star Spangled Banner. How's that?"

"Oh, I knew you would have the perfect cake. I'll take it and a loaf of oat bread with Bluegrass for my husband, please."

"Got it. Anything else?"

"No thanks. I'll be over in three hours to pick it up."

Jeremy sighed internally. How do you tell the First Lady when to pick up her bread? "Can you make it in two? I had hoped to be gone by then."

"Two? I suppose I could have one of the staff pick it up by then. Thanks so much." The line clicked to a busy signal.

If he hurried, he could have her order ready to go into the oven before the others had finished. He pulled out a mixing bowl and whipped together the ingredients for the cake and then the bread, but he left out the baking power and yeast. His bread rose on the beats of a song, none of that artificial stuff.

He had discovered long ago that starting with a certain rhythm had an effect upon the rising, and by playing a particular song, the spirit of the melody would permeate the dough. People marveled how their lives burst into the emotions of the songs when they bit into the breads. People came from miles around to purchase his confections.

After mixing, he put the oat loaf into a soundproof chamber, sat down at his drum set, and rolled out the beats for "The Star Spangled Banner." As each beat rapped upon the snare, bulges of dough would push into the air. Within ten minutes the cake had risen to a fluffy height that any red-blooded American would be proud of.

Jeremy wiped his forehead. He had been doing this all day long; he needed something to pick him up. He reached over to his personal stash of breads and pulled out a Hard Rock muffin. That should do the trick.

While he chewed the rockin' bread, he pushed the cake into the oven and pulled out the dough from the soundproof box. After licking his fingers of the last crumbs, he sat down to inject the oat bread with a snappy bluegrass beat. If only he had an extra set of arms to play the banjo too.

Before he could put stick to skin, the front door bell rang. He hurried to the counter to find a man with a half-eaten loaf of sweet bread.

"Yes, Sir?"

"You see this loaf? Does it look eaten to you?"

"Well, part of it."

"It didn't work. I thought she liked country music, but she asked for a divorce."

"I told you 'Take This Job and Shove it,' might not be the most romantic piece you could find."

"I don't care, I want my money back!"

"You're missing a great opportunity here. Why don't you take this to work and share it?"

His eyes squinted at Jeremy, then relaxed as they scanned upward. "Hum, that has some merit. I could probably get a raise."

"Meanwhile, maybe you should go with my original suggestion and get another loaf infused with 'You Are So Beautiful.'"

He nodded. "Sold."

"I'll have it tomorrow. I'm maxed out tonight."

They exchanged money and Jeremy returned to his set. The loaf of bread for the President of the United States of America lay flat on the kneading board. An idea formed in his mind.

"Bluegrass indeed! I've noticed your graying hair and haggard look, Mr. President. I know just what you need." Jeremy rapped out the discontented beats of "Take This Job and Shove It" as the bubbling bread filled with musical life.

Clever Love

The forest beckoned Jal'ra to return. His elvish kinsmen romped among those branches. Memories of children chasing squirrels and each other demanded he not leave. No longer sensing the familiar melody of the trees resonating in his heart didn't help either.

But the woman. Every night she broke through his dreams crying for help. Crying for him. Her slender beauty, her brown, flowing hair shimmering in the moonlight, drew him to her as much as the dream's madness pushed him from his home.

He gritted his teeth, breathed deep to clear his mind, and forced himself to face the barren landscape. At least it felt barren compared to the forest. A dirt road cut its way across fields of grass, dotted by an occasional tree, bush, or bunch of wild flowers. The sun felt hotter with no canopy to shield him. He sniffed. And the air had lost that leafy smell he'd grown to love. It smelled empty.

But the road pointed to a walled city resting on a foothill about a day's journey away. A snow-capped mountain provided a backdrop, causing Jal'ra to admit beauty existed outside the woods. Maybe he'd find the new world welcoming.

He shoved the narrow-brimmed, leather hat down over his ears. Reports of human unpredictability indicated his best bet would be secrecy. Jal'ra adjusted his pack and stepped toward the distant scene. One step at a time. Then one mile. He passed deer grazing, birds singing, and crossed a couple of streams. But the vision of her haunted him, even in this bright land.

The sun kissed the horizon as he strolled through the city's thick gateway. Men loaded a cart at a shop to his left. Children played hide-n-seek to his right. Dust swirled around him and he sneezed. This certainly wasn't the forest.

Jal'ra spotted a sign among the buildings that read *River Inn*. He entered the wood-frame structure and after acquiring a room, decided the best way to discover news about the girl was to eat in the common room.

After stowing his pack, he slipped down the hall and followed the smell of food. Round, wooden tables greeted him. Men filled most of them, but a few women mingled here and there. The drone of voices buzzed through the air. Smoke from pipes hovered under the ceiling, while barkeeps toted mugs of ale and food among the crowd.

Jal'ra approached where four men conversed. "Mind if I join you gents?"

One with a heavy black beard craned his neck around and studied him. "You ain't from around here, are ya?"

Jal'ra smiled. Locals would be most likely to know enough to help him. "No, sir. I am not. My name's Jal."

"And where do you hail from, Jal?"

Jal'ra thought for a second. "The other side of the Great Woods."

The man smiled and lifted his mug. "Aye, that be a ways off, not to mention the trip through the woods. You're lucky to have come out alive with all those elves about."

Jal'ra clenched his jaw and hoped they didn't notice.

"Have a seat. My name's Greg. This here is John, Dan, and Stan."

They each shook Jal'ra's hand. Jal'ra seated himself and called for food. Soon a barkeep placed a bowl of stew, stale bread, and a mug of ale before him.

Greg swallowed a bite and downed it with a gulp of ale. "So, Jal, what brings you so far to the fair city of Rivertown?"

Jal'ra wondered how honest he should be, but he'd not find the information he needed by keeping his mission a secret. "I'm hunting for a girl."

Dan, a slender-faced man with the bare hint of a goatee on his chin, laughed. "Son, you never hunt for a girl. They hunt you and make you think you're hunting them."

Jal'ra chuckled. "You're closer to the truth than you know for I've never met this woman, yet she appears in my dreams every night. I'm most certainly being hunted."

Stan thrust his mug toward Jal'ra. "Tell us what she looks like, lad. Maybe we can help ya."

Jal'ra stared at the ceiling as he talked. "She has hauntingly beautiful, coal-black eyes. Flowing brown hair cascades over her shoulders. Her angular face, high cheeks, and a discreet nose display an enticing smile upon reddish lips."

John shook his head. "You know how many fit that description in this city alone?"

He nodded. "But she does have one unique mark upon her left cheek: a star-shaped birthmark."

Their eyes grew wide, and they glanced at each other.

"You know this woman?" Jal'ra asked.

Greg nodded. "Aye. She's the king's daughter. She's said to be born with such a mark."

"The king's daughter?" Jal'ra's heart sank. How could he marry her? As soon as the king discovered his secret, he'd be kicked out of town, if not hung.

John slapped him on the back. "Don't fret, Jal. Everyone has a chance to win her hand. Have you heard of the contest?"

Jal'ra shook his head. "I'm afraid I know little of the local news here."

John swallowed a gulp of ale. "The king has proclaimed that anyone who passes his test will win his daughter's hand. No one has succeeded."

Dan pointed at Jal'ra. "You should go to the king tomorrow and try. I can tell she has a grip on your heart."

"Aye, she does." Jal'ra swallowed the last of the stew and drained his mug. "Thanks for the company, but I must turn in."

They grunted their acknowledgment, and Jal'ra left for his room. He lay upon his bed and lamented his luck. If the girl had been a pauper, he would have had a chance, but not the king's daughter.

His thoughts drifted into dreams.

Jal'ra jerked up in his bed, breathing hard. Images of the girl wooed him in his deepest sleep. Despite the impossibility of winning her love, she still demanded his attention.

He poured water into a cup and wetted his throat as he stared at the faint glow of the sun behind the mountains. He could do nothing else but search her out, even if it meant his death. No, he would be clever. He would fool the king and pass his test. Once married, the king would have to accept him. The king's pride would never allow anyone to know he'd been tricked.

Jal'ra slipped on a black velvet shirt, laced with frills diving into a v-neck. A tan, leather vest covered the shirt, and finished the ensemble with a pair of black, drawstring trousers. Then he pulled a jar from his pack: vanishing cream. He rubbed enough on the tips of his ears to hide the points. He'd bought it from a master herbalist in the woodland community, who had sprinkled it with the right combination of elven magic. He closed the lid and placed it in his pack.

He double-checked his appearance in the mirror. Yes, the ears appeared human. Now he could forgo the hat, which would have to come off before the king. He slid into his boots and left.

Jal'ra strolled through the streets and crowds. An occasional wagon caused people to make way for it, and children chased each other along the roadway. These people would change any forest they inhabited.

Jal'ra approached the gate of the castle. Two guards in mail and armor, bearing a shield and spear each, lowered their spears across the heavy, oak door. "What is your business with the king?" one of the guards asked.

"I'm here to accept the king's challenge, and gain his daughter's hand in marriage."

The guards glanced at each other and shared a smile. The one on the left turned to the door and opened it. "Follow me."

A musty smell attacked Jal'ra, as their feet and the guard's clanging armor echoed among the stone walls and high ceiling. They stopped before a high, split door, carved with grapevines and the symbol of a lion in the center.

The hinges creaked as the guard opened it and entered. Jal watched through the partially open door.

The guard stopped before the king and queen at a table off to the side. "Your royal Highness, the commoner Jal wishes an audience with you."

"And what is the business Jal wishes to speak about?"

"To gain your daughter's hand in marriage."

The king smiled and sat upon his throne. "He may approach the king."

Jal'ra entered at the guard's request and stepped lightly along a red rug stretching from the door to the dais. Columns paralleled the carpet, separating side rooms lined with tables and chairs. Six armored guards stood before each pillar, swords drawn, points on the marble floor, and their hands resting upon the hilts. Jal'ra stopped at the base of the dais and bowed before the king.

"You may arise and state your request." The king rested his fingertips against each other.

Jal'ra stood up. "Your Highness, I understand any man who wishes to win your daughter's hand in marriage has but to pass a test. I would request, with your permission, to undergo this test."

The king tapped his fingers together. "Very well. Go to the address the guard will give you and collect the eighty pounds the woman owes in back-taxes. If you bring me the money, then I will give you my daughter."

Jal'ra's wanted to leap to the task now, but restrained himself. This would be easier than he'd thought. He had expected to slay some dragon or such. "I will do as you request, your Highness."

The king waved his hand. "You are dismissed. Don't bother returning without the money unless you enjoy the whip and the guillotine."

Jal'ra bowed and hurried out the door.

As Jal'ra approached the location the guard had given him, he blinked. He stared at a fragile one-room shack. Rotting wood and a perceptible lean warned it could collapse at any moment. A field of weeds surrounded the dwelling. Five kids, dirty and loud, chased each other around the small building.

Jal'ra glanced at the notes he'd written down. No other building lay close enough to fit the directions. This had to be it. He crept to the door. The kids all skidded to a halt and stared at him as if he'd come from another planet. Jal'ra worried that his vanishing cream might have worn off.

Jal'ra waved at them and smiled. They all laughed, then fled by him for another trip around their house.

Jal'ra shook his head and knocked on the door. It gave with each hit, dust and splinters of wood falling to the ground.

The door opened. A woman fixed her eyes on him and frowned. Random strands of hair jutted out from under a head-covering. "What do you want?"

Jal'ra opened his mouth, but paused. How could he ask this woman, who obviously couldn't support her own family, to cough up eighty pounds for taxes? He seriously doubted she possessed the money. But he could only ask. "Ma'am, I regret asking this, but—"

"You want to marry the king's daughter, do ya now?" She frowned at him.

"I came to collect the taxes you owe."

She laughed. "That means you want to marry the king's daughter. The king always sends them to me, you know. Each one discovers there's no way to get money from me."

Jal'ra let his shoulders sag. "Why?"

She laughed again and held out her arms. "What do you see around you? Not even this old house could garner such a price."

Jal'ra scratched his head. "Then how did you end up owing so much money, if you have nothing?"

She pointed to the field behind her house. "One year my husband goes limp while workin' the harvest. All the money from that year's crop, what had been harvested, went to paying the doctors. There was none left for taxes, and we've made little since. I earn what I can as a seamstress."

Jal'ra rested his chin in the palm of his hand, tapping his finger upon his lips. "Why didn't you hire workers to keep the field going?"

"I didn't have enough to feed workers until the harvest money would come. I've barely kept my family going." She waved her hands around her. "See all this? This is what we've got. Take whatever you think will satisfy the king." She grunted then shut the door.

Jal'ra strolled back to the road, then turned around and glanced at the field. Weeds, dotted with broken stalks of long dead plants, danced to the beat of the breeze. He wondered why weeds could grow so easily, without any attention and watering, but the things people needed for living required effort and labor.

He smiled. Of course! What a perfect solution. He removed a vial from his pack and circled the field. As he did, he spilled a drop of the liquid onto the ground. Once he'd finished circumscribing the land, he stood at its edge and sang a song:

Wiggling, squiggling, swimming tadpoles,
Pop out arms, fingers, legs, and toes.
Conversion is nature's way of growing.
Fuzzy, bending, rolling caterpillar,
Hiding in a cocoon at the miller's.
Conversion is nature's way of growing.
Weeds so profuse, so worthless and dumb,
We sing that wheat you would become.
Conversion is nature's way of growing.
Effect the change through each non-plowing.

As Jal'ra sang, the weeds shimmered, shook, and warped into golden wheat. Jal'ra grabbed a harvesting blade by the side of the house, gathered a bundle in his left arm, and cut it lose from the ground.

He stepped back to the front door and banged on it. The woman saw him and frowned. "Go pester someone who cares. I've got..." She froze and stared at the wheat. "Where did you get that?"

Jal'ra stood straight. "If you don't mind, ma'am, I'll have the king's guards come by and pick up the rest later. There should be enough left you can sell to hire out some help."

She scowled. "I'm no fool." She pushed past him. "You saw the field. I've no wheat, none for..." She rounded the corner of the house. Her jaw dropped open. "For years." She turned toward Jal'ra, her eyes wide. "Where did this come from?"

Jal'ra tossed his free hand into the air. "Weeds, wheat. Hard to tell the difference between them sometimes. But let me know when you've baked bread with it. It'll beat the stuff at the inn, no doubt."

She stared at the field and waved her hand at it. "Take all you want for the king."

Jal'ra nodded and tipped his hat. "Until next time."

He slipped back onto the road. His lips couldn't help but grin. "One king's daughter soon to be mine!"

Jal'ra stood before the king. A servant scanned papers, then met the king's eyes. "Aye, your Highness. The men have collected all that the woman owed."

The king focused on Jal'ra. "How did you do this? The lady was destitute."

Jal'ra forced himself to not smile. "Your Highness, I simply aided the poor lady to revive her business. Once she had the means, she could pay."

The king rubbed his chin. "You're a clever one, you are."

"Then if I may be so bold, your Highness..." He bowed. "When should I expect to obtain your daughter's hand in marriage?"

"You may be so bold, but I'll be bolder." The king leaned forward in his throne. "Any future royal family member must know not only how to collect money, but how to use it. I'll have my keeper of the books place at your disposal ten thousand pounds. I expect you to invest it. If within a month you do not have more than you started out with, you cannot have my daughter as a wife."

Jal'ra frowned. "I beg your pardon, your Highness, but I thought there was only one test?"

The king yawned and covered his mouth. "I've changed my mind."

Jal'ra grumbled inside, but what could he do? "Yes, your Highness. I will do as you command."

"One other thing." The king pointed at Jal'ra. "Should you lose my money, you'll stay in prison until it's paid back."

Jal'ra nodded, but refrained from saying anything further. No sense offending his future father-in-law.

A guard motioned for Jal'ra to follow him. They threaded their way through several echoing hallways until they arrived at a room. Rows of desks filled the space, each holding an abacus, quill, inkwell, and sheets of parchment.

The guard stopped before one desk; the man sitting there raised his head. The guard placed a hand on Jal'ra's shoulder. "The king has charged this man to invest ten thousand pounds on his behalf during the next month."

The man raised an eyebrow. "He's never given me such a charge."

"You never accomplished the first test."

The bookkeeper grumbled. "All right." He turned to Jal'ra. "Do you wish to have the money now?"

Jal'ra shook his head. "I'll wait until I know what to do with it."

The man nodded. "I'll be here when you're ready."

The guard focused on Jal'ra. "Remember, you only have a month. If you wait too long, there won't be time for it to mature."

Jal'ra stifled a laugh. "Thank you for your timely investment advice. I'll return within the next couple of days for the money."

The guard led Jal'ra out of the king's castle. Jal'ra returned to the inn. He entered the common room, and upon seeing his new friends, sat beside them to eat.

Greg patted him on the back. "Good to see you again. So, how is it going with the girl?"

"Doing well so far. I passed the first test, but the king gave me another."

Dan whistled. "No one's passed that first test. You're a clever one, you are."

John rubbed his chin. "There's more than one test?"

Stan swallowed a bite. "What is the second test?"

"The king's given me ten thousand pounds to invest. If I make a profit, I'll get the girl. If not, I'm in prison, probably for the rest of my life."

John grunted. "Sounds like the safest thing to do is put it in a bank. With the interest it earns, you'd win."

Jal'ra nodded. "A good plan. Where's the bank?"

John's face sagged. "*Rivertown* doesn't have one. You'd have to travel two days each way to *King's Dale*."

Jal'ra frowned. "Too risky. Not only could bandits steal the money, but if something delays me, I may not return in time." Jal'ra considered the king could have arranged for such misfortunes to befall him, expecting him to seek investments in the major cities of the land. The king hid something, Jal'ra was sure, but what he didn't know.

Greg laughed. "If I had it, I'd end up prison for sure. Because I'd spend it!"

Dan lifted his mug. "And all on ale, no less!"

John shook his head. "It would be tempting to use it for myself. Times are hard of late, and taxes keep going higher."

Greg turned to Jal'ra. "So, have you figured out how you'll be investing it?"

Jal'ra patted Greg on the back. "Yes. You gents have provided me with an idea."

Dan lifted a bite of beef on his spoon. "You're not going to spend it on ale, I hope."

Jal'ra nodded. "In a manner of speaking, yes. Ale and much more."

They stared at Jal'ra for a few seconds before Greg spoke. "I'll come and visit you in prison when I can."

Jal'ra rose and bowed. "Fear not. Prison food I'll not be eating. Goodnight." Jal'ra left for his room.

Jal'ra stood before the bookkeeper. "I'm ready to receive the money."

The man cocked his head. "Have a plan, do we?"

"Yes, I do."

"And what is this plan?"

Jal'ra shook his head. "That's between me and the king."

"Very well." He rose with a huff, then entered the king's vaults. In a few minutes, he returned with two handfuls of bills. Jal'ra received them and shoved them into a pouch belted to his hip.

The bookkeeper shoved paper, a feather, and an inkwell toward Jal'ra. "Sign here." He pointed to an empty line.

Jal'ra signed and left the building. He scanned up and down the street. Spotting a butcher shop, he entered the door and stood at the counter. The smell of blood and flesh tickled his nose.

A muscular man dressed in a bloody apron approached him. "What can I do for ya?"

Jal'ra smiled. "It's more what can I do for you. I have a business proposition for you, if you're willing to consider it."

He shrugged. "Get on with it, then. I've work to do."

"The king has commissioned me to distribute money to whomever I see fit. I'm willing to put one thousand pounds into your hands today, if you'll agree to the following requirements: you must use the money to either lower your prices and, or hire more employees, for at least a month."

The man rubbed his hands on his apron, staring at the wall for a moment. "And the king has placed no other restrictions on this?"

"No. I speak for him on this matter."

"I think I can do that. I do need the help, and lower prices could result in more sales." He reached out a hand. "You've got a deal."

Jal'ra shook it. "Deal." He pulled a thousand pounds from his pouch and placed it on the counter. "I'll check back to ensure you are using it as promised. If I find otherwise, you'll risk imprisonment."

He nodded. "I understand."

Jal'ra found nine more businesses: a blacksmith, a tanner, the inn, the laundry cleaners, the farm co-op, the town crier association, a sword maker, a cleaning service, and the last thousand he divided between ten out-of-work men, to start their own businesses.

The month drifted slowly by. Jal'ra kept tabs on the various places he'd placed the money. Business picked up for each, and several who were to start businesses served a thriving clientele. When he ate with his friends, they exhibited a more optimistic attitude as well.

The time arrived to appear before the king once again. Jal'ra requested the bookkeeper's presence.

The king drummed his fingers on the armrest of the throne. The queen sat in another chair to the side. "So, how did you invest my money?"

Jal'ra bowed. "Your Highness, after careful thought, I gave the money to select businesses and people."

The king jumped to his feet and pointed a finger at Jal'ra. "You gave my money away? Don't you know those are the very people I taxed to get that money?"

"I beg your forgiveness, your Highness, but what would you have me invest in, if not your own kingdom?"

He threw up his hands. "There are other kingdoms, other lords. There is only so much money here." He addressed the guards. "Take him to prison!"

A pair of guards moved toward Jal'ra. Jal'ra held up a hand. "If you'd give me but a minute more of your Majesty's valuable time, you should hear what your keeper of the books has to say."

The king clenched his jaw, but then nodded and sat down, scowling as he did.

Jal'ra turned to the bookkeeper. "How much taxes did you collect this month compared to the last?"

He smiled. "We collected twenty thousand pounds more this month than last."

The king's eyes grew wide. "Twenty thousand!"

One of the guards spoke up. "Not only that, your Highness, but the rumors of a riot have died off and crime has decreased noticeably over previous months."

The king scratched his beard. "Well, aren't you the clever one. I'd never figured I'd get more money by giving it away."

Jal'ra bowed. "Standard market economics, your Highness. Ten thousand pounds goes a long ways in this city."

The king remained silent for a moment. "Well then, you've proved yourself to me. You may have my daughter's hand in marriage. Only one condition left do you need to fulfill."

Jal'ra groaned inwardly. "And what may that be, your Highness?"

"You must retrieve her from her captor. She resides in a cave guarded by a dragon who fell in love with her and will not let her go."

Jal'ra shook his head. He knew a dragon would come into this at some point. But he'd come this far; he couldn't stop now. "Provide the location of this cave, and I will rescue your daughter."

The king pointed at a knight and wiggled his finger. The knight approached and bowed before the king. "Yes, your Highness?"

"Go with Jal, provide him a weapon, and show him the location of the cave. Once there, leave him and return."

"It will be as you wish, your Highness." The knight led Jal'ra out of the king's hall and to the armory. Swords, axes, lances, spears, maces, bows and arrows, and other weapons lined the shelves. "Which weapon do you desire?"

Jal'ra slid his fingers along the edge of a sword's blade. "I'll only require one weapon." He pointed to a corner. "That sling."

The knight laughed. "You could barely kill a rabbit with that, much less a dragon."

Jal'ra smiled. "That's between me and the king."

The knight shook his head and chuckled. "So be it." He pulled the sling from its hook and placed it in Jal'ra's hand. "Keep in mind, this dragon's hide is impenetrable. An arrow from a crossbow wouldn't dent it, much less a rock from this sling."

"I'll keep that in mind." Jal'ra turned and left the castle, the knight pointing the way.

They left the city gates, walking on a road heading north. The mountains towered over them, snow capped and foreboding. The forest grew dense, and underbrush ensured no one left the road. Jal'ra breathed in their leafy scent, refreshing his spirits.

Jal'ra pointed at the mountains. "How far?"

"The cave's about half a day's journey."

"Tell me, have you fought this dragon before?"

He smiled. "Oh yes. Twice, as a matter of fact."

"And you've lived to tell the tale?"

"Aye. The first time I...," and the knight spent the rest of the trip relating his tales, flourishes and all.

As the sun rose high in the sky, they approached the base of the foothills. Jal'ra wiped his brow and noticed a trail that led into the forest.

The knight nodded toward it. "You'll find the cave at the end of that path. May your luck be better than mine." He stared at the sling, then laughed again, before heading back to the city.

Jal'ra raised the flask of water to his lips and drank. "Nothing for it but to go see this dragon."

He proceeded onto the path. The trees vibrated with a different tune than what he'd grown up with. Yet, they possessed a deep knowledge, as deep as any he'd encountered before. He longed to jump through their branches and commune with them, but he couldn't afford to waste time. Singing with the birds would come later, if he could save the woman of his dreams.

He spent at least an hour working his way among branches and brush as the trail wound here and there, climbing up the side of the hill. A clearing pulled into view; Jal'ra crept toward the edge.

A dragon lay in front of a cave. Its body shimmered in the sunlight, as its blue-green bulk rose and fell to the steady breathing of the beast. A long tail wound around its feet, and a snout exhaled caustic fumes below eyes closed in sleep.

Jal'ra skittered across the grassy knoll upon a cushion of air. He hopped upon the creature's back and glided across it until he stood over its head. He knelt and found a hair protruding from the dragon's ear. Jal'ra retrieved a small ball from his pouch. The liquid inside sloshed as he opened a door on its top, yanked the hair from the dragon's ear, and shoved it into the ball.

The dragon jerked; its eyes flashed open. It wiggled its snout and sniffed. Dragon-scented vapor escaped from the ball in Jal'ra's hand. The dragon's nose sniffed harder.

Jal'ra settled the ball into the sling and swung it around five times before releasing it. The ball sailed over a hill, leaving a thick trail of smoke in its wake.

Jal'ra leaped off the dragon as it lifted its head and stretched out its tail and wings to steady itself. Jal'ra hid behind a tree trunk. The dragon's nose led its body around, pointing in the direction of the smoke-trail.

"Another dragon? Here?" The beast roared and flames poured from its mouth. It extended its wings and lifted from the ground, blowing Jal'ra's hair with each beat. The dragon followed the vapor-trail over the hill.

Jal'ra jumped from behind the tree as soon as the dragon had left. He raced into the cave, the hard rock poking his feet. A light grew ahead of him a few feet in. He entered a cavern. A ragged hole at the top let in sunlight, illuminating the dry stalagmites and stalactites decorating the white-brown walls and floors.

He didn't have time to search the whole area. The dragon could return at any time once it realized the smell led to nothing. Jal'ra cupped his hands. "Hello, anyone in here?"

A head rose from a corner of the room. Eyes blinked amidst brown hair, cascading over her shoulders. Her eyes widened, and she dashed among the rocks until she stood before Jal'ra.

She wore a tattered and dirty dress. At one time, it would have dazzled and accented her beauty. Her slender form heaved heavy breaths. "You've come. I knew you would."

Jal'ra grabbed her hand. "Follow me."

She nodded and together they fled from the cave and into the woods along the trail. A roar sounded in the distance. Her eyes grew dark. "You didn't kill the dragon?"

"No, I merely tricked it into thinking another dragon lurked nearby."

"Then our escape may only be temporary." She leaped over stones and branches as gracefully as a doe.

Jal'ra thought her as surefooted as she was beautiful. He glanced back over his shoulder to see the dragon circling over his lair. "We'll have to go into the woods to hide."

"But the dragon can smell us out."

"Trust me." Jal'ra directed them to a low section of underbrush and they pushed through the branches. Water drops plopped against his cheeks, causing him to stare into the sky.

He'd been so focused on their escape that he'd failed to notice the storm clouds marching his way. Thunder cracked in the distance. The dragon flew toward them, searching for her scent.

Jal'ra stopped. "Wait." He examined the enticing brown threads of her hair. "I need a strand of your hair."

"For what?"

"You'll see. It'd take too long to explain." He held out his hand.

She nodded, grabbed a hair, and winced as she pulled. Then she placed the thread into his hand.

The dragon circled over them, roaring, zeroing in on their location. It wouldn't be long before it would start burning the forest to chase them out.

Jal'ra pulled out another ball and placed the hair in it. Smoke floated from the device. He positioned it in the sling, but this time he sang as he spun it faster and faster:

Roll a ball
Roll a fall
Smell me here
Smell me there
Just as long
As you're gone!

He released the sling and the ball flew into the air. It soared toward the mountain peaks, disappearing into the clouds hovering around their tops.

The dragon circled over the pair, then roared and chased the smell toward the sky.

Rain sputtered, then poured as they stood among the trees, soaking them both.

Her eyes widened.

Jal'ra examined her. "What's wrong?"

She pointed at him. "You're an elf."

His heart sank. The rain must have washed away the vanishing cream. But who did he think he fooled? She would have discovered the truth at some point. But to have come this close... He wrapped his arm around a trunk and whispered for mercy.

She peered under his bowed head. "When I saw you in my dream, promising to rescue me, I couldn't get you off my mind."

"Nor you off mine." He sucked in a deep breath. "That's why I came, even though I am an elf."

She smiled, and he could smell her smile through the rain. "Don't be sad. I like elves, myself." She pulled her hair back to reveal pointed ears.

Jal'ra let his jaw drop. Then he grinned. "You're an elf too?"

She nodded. "Half elf, half human. My mother is an elf. The king, however, wanted to keep my race a secret. So he entrusted me into the care of this dragon."

He blinked. "Your father gave you to this dragon?"

"Yes. The dragon would devour anyone who came to rescue me. But you have outwitted my guardian. You must be a very clever elf."

"So I'm told." Jal'ra restrained his exuberance so not to appear a fool in front of her. He thought a moment as water trickled down his cheeks. "How many in the kingdom know elven blood runs in your veins?"

She leaned against a tree. "The king, the queen, and the knight who negotiated the deal with the dragon."

Jal'ra rubbed his chin. "I would like to ask your father for your hand in marriage."

A smile graced her face, but quickly died away. "He'll deny me as his own."

"But men at the inn told me my description was the king's daughter?"

"He's described me to them, all except my ears and race, because no one's ever seen me. They wouldn't know any different."

Jal'ra touched the star birthmark on her wet cheek with a finger. "So, everyone can identify you, but most don't know you're an elf?"

She nodded. "That's right."

He glanced around the trees. "Being part elf, have you ever climbed the trees?"

Her eyes sparkled. "That's where I feel the most at home."

"Me too. Let's reach the city through the trees. Less chance the dragon will find us."

"Lead on, my clever elf."

He bounded up the rain-scented trunk and she followed. He'd never felt freer as he shot around tree branch and limb with her at his side, and dew from heaven blessing their shared joy. The trees rejoiced with vibrating melodies around them. They raced the birds and squirrels, and dodged a sloth. As the moon hung in the night sky, and stars rolled across the blackness like distant candles, they lit upon the ground not far from the city gates.

Jal'ra dug in his pack and pulled out a cloak. "Wear this. The hood will hide your face, so no one will recognize you. Tomorrow, I'll approach the king and ask to marry you."

She slipped the cloak on and pulled the hood over her head. "Don't you think we should introduce each other first?"

He slapped his forehead. "I'm sorry. In all the excitement I forgot." He held his hand out, palm up. "My name is Jal'ra."

She placed her hand in his. "And I'm called Serenade, Seren for short."

He pulled her hand up and gently kissed it. "A most appropriate name, for your beauty sings a breathtaking song."

She blushed.

The next morning, Jal'ra entered the king's hall. He stopped before the king and bowed. The queen sat at the table by the wall.

The king frowned. "I'm surprised you've returned."

"Did you fear the dragon had devoured me?"

"When my knight said you selected a sling for your weapon, yes. The fact you are still here and without my daughter means you're a coward. Thus I'm doubly surprised that you stand before me now, knowing I would imprison you at best or kill you at worst."

"I'm training the dragon."

The king raised an eyebrow. "Training it?"

Jal'ra cracked a smile. "I've been teaching him to play fetch."

The king growled. "If you've rescued my daughter, then bring her forth. Otherwise, I'll command the guards to lock you away."

Jal'ra shook his index finger. "If I bring her forth now, a certain minor fact could become—shall we say—public knowledge." Jal'ra raised an eyebrow.

The king's jowls sagged and his eyes stared at Jal'ra for a moment. Then as if shaking off thoughts, he blinked and faced his chief guard. "Everyone but Jal'ra and the queen, out."

"Yes, your Highness," each said in turn and marched out the door. One hooded figure walked down the aisle. She stopped beside Jal'ra. Once the last of the guards exited and shut the door, Serenade pulled back her hood and beamed a smile at her father.

The king stared at her, his eyes wide. "You did rescue her."

"And you failed to tell me one critical fact." Jal'ra pulled her hair back, revealing a pointed ear. "She's an elf."

The king sank back into his chair and rubbed his forehead.

Jal'ra frowned. "We have a problem. I'm not in the habit of marrying elves. Yet if I refuse her now, you will be disgraced among your subjects. But if I marry her and live here, people will eventually find out what she is.

"To prevent either disaster from befalling you, I'm willing to marry her under one condition."

The king's knuckled turned white as he gripped the throne's armrests. He said through clenched teeth, "And what condition is that?"

"That you give me the northern forest and all therein as my and my descendant's kingdom in perpetuity."

The king leaped from his throne. "What? Are you out of your mind!"

Jal'ra shrugged and turned to Serenade. "Are you hungry, my dear? I have some friends at the pub who are dying to meet you."

The king slammed his fist on the armrest and plopped back into his seat. "All right! You can have it, but if anyone discovers her race before I die, you will lose your kingdom." The king sighed. "And one other condition: that you'll not prevent me from hunting on the land."

Jal'ra grinned. "Done." He slid out a parchment and unrolled it. "I took the liberty to draw up the legal documents last night." He wrote in the additional demands and handed it to the king.

The king called for his advisers to verify its validity after Serenade replaced her hood. As the advisers gathered around the document, the queen rose from her seat and briskly stepped toward the two.

A smile graced her face, and her eyes glowed as she met Serenade's gaze. The two wrapped their arms around each other in a long hug.

Jal'ra pointed at the queen as they pulled apart. "So, are you...?"

The queen pushed the edge of her head-covering back enough to reveal pointed ears. Serenade cupped her hands and whispered into her mother's ear. The queen's eyes grew round and a grin spread across her face. She whispered, "I'll never say a word about this."

After the advisers agreed that the terms were satisfactory and honest, the king shook his head and signed the decree. "The wedding will be in three days."

Jal'ra wanted to leap for joy, but bowed instead. "Thank you, your Highness."

Serenade beamed a smile first at her father, then at Jal'ra. A scent of racing expectation wafted from her.

The king sat upon his throne. "But you may regret the deal in the end. Those woods are so thick, you'll have a hard time clearing them."

Jal'ra smiled. "That's between me and the woods."

The edges of the king's mouth twitched. "You are a clever one. May your love be just as clever."

Jal'ra bowed. "More clever than you know, your Highness. More clever than you know."

About the Author

R. L. Copple's interest in speculative fiction started at an early age, after reading "Runaway Robot" by Lester Del Ray. Many others followed by Asimov, Bradbury, Heinlein, Tolkien, C. S. Lewis, among others. He has written for religious purposes but started writing speculative fiction in 2005. Infinite Realities marks his first book, a fantasy novella published in November 2007. His second book and first novel, Transforming Realities, hit the shelves March 2009. He has been published in several magazines. More info can be found at author's web site, http://www.rlcopple.com.

Twitter: http://www.twitter.com/rlcopple

Facebook: http://www.facbook.com/rlcopple

Blog: http://blog.rlcopple.com

Made in the USA
Columbia, SC
02 November 2021